"Guess this means we'll be working together."

"I guess so." Chelsea's chest tied up in all kinds of knots. Was this good news or bad? Her hand shook as she secured the last string of Christmas lights, leaving a good six inches dangling free.

"I knew Denny was adding a pediatrician to the practice, but I didn't know it was you," Michael said.

"It's been planned for a long time. Denny was my mom's doctor."

"I understand." For a moment, his friendly but cool reserve vanished and the understanding she read in the shadows of his gentle gaze made her defenses stumble. He was a good man, and the smallest of wishes flickered to life against her will, wishes for a strong, good man she could count on.

Not going to happen, she told herself with a twist of regret.

Not that she wanted the hassle of a relationship, she told herself firmly and wrestled the wish away. She had a plan. No involvements, no romance, no wishing for a love that could not be.

Her No Man plan.

Jillian Hart grew up on her family's homestead, where she helped raise cattle, rode horses and scribbled stories in her spare time. After earning her English degree from Whitman College, she worked in travel and advertising before selling her first novel. When Jillian isn't working on her next story, she can be found puttering in her rose garden, curled up with a good book or spending quiet evenings at home with her family.

God is the Lord, and He has given us light.
—*Psalms* 118:27

To Chelsea Tripp, DVM, DACVIM

Chapter One

Snow tumbled from an unforgiving sky, icy against her cheek as Chelsea McKaslin knelt in the small town's cemetery. The marker was simple, the white marble hard to read in the falling twilight and the accumulating snow. She swept away the fluffy inches of flakes from the gravestone with her fingertips, her hand-knit crimson mittens a vivid splash of color in a white, gray and dark evening. Ever since her mother had passed on, the world hadn't seemed as kind or as colorful.

"Hi, Mom." She laid pink carnations on the headstone, where the name Jessica Elizabeth McKaslin was etched, beloved wife and mother. "It's me, Chelsea. I've missed coming to see you, but I did what you asked. I finished my residency. I stuck it out. It was tough, the last thing I wanted to do after you were gone, but I did it."

More than anything she wished—she prayed—

that her mother could hear her. That her words could lift through the airy snowfall and rise up to heaven as if on angels' wings. Her faith had been tested over the two years of Mom's sickness and death, but it remained strong. She still believed. Somewhere her mother was looking down at her and smiling. Her love lived on. Maybe it was in the soft brush of snowflakes against Chelsea's cheek or the whisper behind the wind, so light it was barely audible. She liked to think so.

"Christmas is not the same without you." She could hope it would be better than last year with the gaping, painful hole in their lives and in their family. No one and nothing could ever fill the void. "Sara Beth and Meg plan to fix our traditional dinner this year. Johanna has her heart set on a tree. We're all pooling our gift money to start a scholarship in your name."

The electronic jingle of her cell penetrated her wool coat's outer pocket. She fumbled for it, the mitten's thickness and the numbing cold making her fingers clumsy. The number on the luminous display came as no surprise.

"I'm almost home," she said, squinting as the snowfall thickened, beating against her face.

"I was worried." Her youngest sister's voice sounded crackly. Reception was terrible because of the storm. "I've been keeping an eye on the clock and the weather report. Half the county roads are closed, and you should have been here twenty minutes ago. Where are you?"

"Safe. I had to stop by and visit Mom."

Johanna's silence said it all. Understanding zoomed across the line, the static unable to diminish the strong bond between them. Chelsea didn't have to explain how she'd been needing this place of connection to their mother.

"The roads are getting worse by the minute," Johanna reminded her gently. "I want you home safely."

"That's my plan." Chelsea was good with plans. They had always been her strong suit.

She took comfort in a logical world, in compiling pro and con lists and puzzling out the road ahead. Once sure of her destination, she gave all she had into getting there. That's how she had gotten accepted to med school and won a coveted residency position. She'd always taken to heart the Bible passage: a man chooses his path and God directs his steps.

"I'm leaving right now," she promised.

"Good, because they are about to close Grimes Road. I thought you might want a heads-up, that is, if you want to sleep in your old bed tonight."

"You know I do." Home. There was no place like it. She'd had her own apartment for years, but her family's piece of the Wyoming rangeland would always be her real home. Full of memories of love and laughter, made more special this time of year. Christmas had always been done right at the McKaslin household. She thought of her mom, how she always used to be waiting to welcome her daughters, cooking and baking up a storm. They all gained ten pounds every visit, especially if they weren't careful.

It was hard to think of opening the front door and not seeing her there. Chelsea pocketed her phone, realizing she was shivering. The arctic cold sliced through her coat like a razor, chilling her to the bone. She faced into the wind, blind as the snowflakes struck her with a worsening fury. She really did need to get home while she could.

Snow squeaked beneath her boots as she hiked around headstones and across the rippled sheen of snow accumulating in the parking lot. Security spotlights glowed like tiny moons hovering overhead, their light eerie and veiled. At least she would get her snow fix. She didn't miss Seattle's gray drizzle, not one bit, as she knocked snow off her car's windows. Home was all she could think about, her sisters waiting for her, the front door swinging open and Johanna launching out of it with a welcoming squeal. *Lord, please see me safely home—*

"Daddy! Daddy!"

A little girl's voice broke into her prayer, a lonely and frightened sound in the thick snowfall. Chelsea froze, heart drumming. She glanced around, but there was no sign of another car as far as she could see, which wasn't far at all. The snow had picked up speed, cutting visibility.

"Daddy!" Shrill this time, sharp as if on the edge of tears. Something was wrong. Was the child alone? Hurt? In danger?

She bolted from her car, trying to gauge where the cry had come from. A little north, she decided, as the snow grabbed at her boots and the wind pushed against her, holding her back. The labored sound of her breathing, her footsteps crunching in the accumulation and the thousand whispering taps of the snowflakes hitting the ground was all she could hear. No other sound from the child.

She definitely hadn't imagined it, but the thickening darkness gave no hint of where the girl might be. Now what did she do? Chelsea swiped snow from her lashes, turning in a slow circle. Maybe she'd gotten disoriented and the child was farther away then she'd thought. Wait—was that something? She held her breath, listening. There it was again, a hiccup, such a small sound.

Thank God she heard it. She kept going, angling toward the graves, until she came across small boot prints. They led her to a little girl sprawled on the ground in the inky shadows.

"Daddy?" she sniffled.

"No, I'm sorry, it's just me." She hit the button

on the miniature flashlight clipped to her key chain—a stocking stuffer from Mom three Christmases ago—and a faint light illuminated the girl. Maybe seven, eight years old. Pale face, big eyes, tears pooling, but they didn't fall. The child was out here all alone? "Hi, I'm Chelsea. What's your name?"

"I'm not supposed to tell strangers that."

"That's right and face it, I'm a stranger. My sisters tell me all the time that I'm really strange." A little humor might make the kid feel more at ease. "But not scary, although this storm is a little scary. I can't see a thing. How about you?"

"No. That's why I fell down." Silken brown wisps peeked out from a bright purple knit hat. The little girl swiped at them with a matching mitten on her good hand. "It was the curb."

"I tripped on it when I got here. Almost fell right on my nose. I'm saying it was the curb's fault, too. Definitely not ours." Chelsea hunkered in, keeping her voice soft. She didn't need her medical degree to see the girl's arm was hurt, or why else would she be cradling it? "You must be here with your family?"

"My daddy." The pooling tears threatened to spill. She was a cutie, with a round face, a sloping nose and a porcelain-doll look. Someone's precious daughter. "I got to pick out the wreath but it was too sad leaving it at the stone."

"I know just what you mean." She thought of the flowers she'd left behind, pushed aside her grief and gave thanks she was a pediatrician. Her training would come in handy. "Now what about your arm? Can you move your fingers?"

"I don't want to." The kid shook her head, scattering snowflakes and locks of molasses. "There's nothing wrong. It's just cold."

"I see." She'd had stubborn patients before. "Is the rest of you cold too, or just your arm?"

"My arm especially. It'll be okay, I just know it." Honest blue eyes looked up into hers, so serious. "I really need my dad."

"I'll help you find him." She'd feel better if she could take a look at that arm, which the girl held gingerly. A sprained wrist? A fracture? The doctor in her was itching to find out. The dad couldn't be far. "Leave it to me. I have three sisters, so I'm really good at hollering. What's his name?"

"Dr. Kramer. I— Well, I guess it's okay to tell you my name. It's Macie."

"It's good to meet you, Macie. I'm Chelsea. Tell you what, I'll holler and we'll follow your tracks back to him, all right?"

"But I don't want to go back. It makes me sad." Macie stayed right where she was, sorrow shining in her blue gaze. "It's cuz my mom is here."

"I'm sorry." Sympathy hit Chelsea so hard, it

left her weak. Tears burned behind her eyes. "My mom is buried here, too. I know just how you feel."

Michael Kramer pressed his gloved hand against the gray marble as if to will what remained of his regret through the cold stone. Icy flecks of snow beat against his face as he fought not to remember his failings as a husband.

"The storm's worsening, Macie." He adjusted the wreath of plastic poinsettias, already dotted with snow. "We'd better get home before the roads close."

No little girl's voice answered. Probably because his daughter was no longer standing behind him. There was nothing but the impression in the snow of her two booted feet. Why hadn't he noticed earlier? Frustrated with himself, he frowned, crinkling his brow. And how many times had he told her not to wander off? He launched to his feet, searching the thick veil of falling snow. No sign of her.

"Macie!" The wind snatched his voice. Snow beat against his coat hood, drowning out all other sounds. Blindly, he swiped snow off his face, noticing the scoop mark in the snow from a child-size mitten. No need to panic. Sunshine, Wyoming, was a safe place for kids, not like Chicago where he'd grown up. She had to be around here somewhere.

"Macie!" He tried again. Still no answer, at least none that he could hear in the rising storm. Not that she wouldn't be easy to find. Just follow the trail.

Her boots cut a visible path into the snow and darkness, roughly heading toward the parking lot. If she'd wanted to leave, she could have just told him. Frustrated, he fisted his hands, teeth chattering in the cold. His daughter was grieving, too. It wasn't easy for him to deal with emotions. Diana, when she'd been alive, had told him that often enough. He feared that made him a terrible father.

A flash of pink penetrated the swirling snow. Macie's coat. What was she doing on the ground and why was someone kneeling over her? He took one look at the bulky navy coat bending over his fallen daughter and the worst thoughts leaped into his mind. Protective fury roared through him. He grew ten feet and his fist closed around the navy coat wearer.

"Get away from her." He hauled the kidnapper to his feet. No one—no one—was going to hurt his daughter.

"Hey! Let go of me." A rather bossy woman yanked her arm out of his grip. "What's wrong with you, buddy?"

A woman? He blinked, the scene coming clear to him. His daughter sitting up, cradling her arm. Macie was hurt. Tears stood in her eyes. Was it this woman's fault? "What are you— I mean, who are you? What's going on here?" he boomed.

"You must be Macie's dad. Good thing you came along. Awesome, right, Macie?" She cast him a quelling look and he felt like an idiot grabbing her like that. The girl was lost. Clearly the woman had been trying to help.

Great. Jump to the wrong conclusion, Michael. Just add it to his long list of idiocies around women. The flare of adrenaline crackling through his blood calmed. Now what did he do? Apologize? Explain that he wasn't a terrible father? All he could see was Macie still on the ground, clutching one arm, pale, shivering and obviously hurt.

"I fell, Daddy." Her lower lip quivered. "It was the curb's fault. That's what Chelsea said."

Chelsea, huh? He bypassed the woman, catching a glimpse of big blue eyes glaring up at him. Her sweet oval face was framed by a hint of light-chestnut-brown hair and topped with a red hat. He ignored the hitch in his chest that made him want to take better notice of her and knelt in front of his daughter. Macie looked fragile and tiny, and his heart seemed to break—but that was impossible because as everyone told him, he didn't have a heart. "Were you daydreaming again? Telling yourself stories?"

"Kinda." She winced. "The snow could be hiding a princess's castle."

"Next time, stay with me, got it?" He gentled his voice, although it still came out gruff. Tenderness wasn't his strong suit either.

Macie nodded. Twin tears trailed down her too-white cheeks.

His poor baby. "C'mon, let's get you in the car."

"No. Chelsea says I need an X-ray." Macie sniffled. "You know why I don't like the emergency room, Daddy?"

Yeah, he knew. He squeezed his eyes shut to hold in the pain. The past flashed like a mosaic—the receptionist bursting into his office with news of an urgent phone call, the mad dash to emergency, seeing Diana still and slight looking in death. His nurse kept Macie in the waiting room. After hearing the sad news the child had sat utterly still, frozen in a room of chaos.

He opened his eyes. Only a second had passed, but it felt like an eternity. "Let me take a look."

"No!" She jerked away, the movement causing pain. More tears fell. "It'll get better. I know it will."

He knew the sound of desperation. He heard it every day in his office, when family members had to face a tough diagnosis. As a specialist, he gave out bad news as a matter of course. He'd had to harden himself so the sadness wouldn't take him down. He had patients to think about, he had to stay uninvolved and rational so he could guide them through a tough and trying time.

He gave thanks that his child was healthy, unlike the others he treated, and wiped at her tears. "Come with me, baby."

"No! I won't go where Mom died." His beautiful daughter hiccupped, upset by memories, which were hard for him, too.

At a loss, he opened his mouth and closed it. He wasn't cut out to be a single father. He wished he were able to do a better job.

Footsteps crunched in the snow behind him. He felt the woman's—Chelsea's—glower as she stomped closer. He hadn't noticed she'd left, but when he spotted two knit blankets folded up in her arms, it touched him.

"She needs to be kept warm." Her blue eyes met his, full of concern, and was that a hint of censure? Or wariness? Her gaze turned kind as she brushed snow off Macie's hat. "If we leave you out here any longer, you are going to turn into a snowman, well, a snowgirl, and that would be bad because then you'd melt away."

"Not if I moved to the north pole." Macie hiccupped, in an effort to hold back her pain. "I could make a house there."

"True. You could live in an igloo. It could be cool." Chelsea rolled her eyes, as if amused by her own pun, and draped one blanket around

Macie's snowy shoulders. "There, now you're ready for transport."

"We're going home, right, Dad?"

"Sorry, baby. I'm worried about your arm."

"The pain is sharp and radiating." Chelsea rose, clutching one remaining blanket. "There's no tingling or numbness in her fingers. No sign of a compound fracture."

"You're a doctor?" It came out gruff and ungrateful-sounding, which isn't what he meant. Not at all.

"That's what they tell me." She glared at him, apparently not willing to share her kindness with him.

Not that he blamed her, grabbing her the way he had. He'd been wrong, but the instinct to protect had been right. Surely she could understand that? Trouble was, he didn't know how to say all that to her. His child was still shivering and in pain, so he gathered her in his arms, keeping his focus where it should be. On his daughter. Her weight in his arms was dear as he stood, cuddling her against his chest. He turned, shielding her from the worst bite of the wind.

"Daddy, promise me." Macie pleaded, fragile and small against him, shaking with cold and pain. "Not the hospital."

"I don't know, baby." Maybe he could think of a solution. The snowstorm worsened, the downfall so thick it hid all signs of the parking lot, but not the woman standing beside him.

"Where's your car?" Chelsea in her navy coat said as she forged ahead. "This way?"

"Yes." He squinted to keep her in sight. She walked easily through the whiteout conditions, graceful as the snowfall. There was something about her that was poetic as the night.

Not that he was given to poetry. He fished his keys from his coat pocket, careful not to jostle Macie. She sniffled against him, fighting her tears. Maybe there was a way to avoid the emergency room. He beeped his remote, and the SUV's lights flashed through the veil of storm. Chelsea surprised him by opening the passenger door, holding it against the gusts of wind so he could settle Macie into her seat. He brushed the snow off her the best he could.

"Here." Chelsea shook out the second blanket and shouldered past him. He caught a faint scent of vanilla and strawberry. Light-chestnut-brown hair spilled out from beneath her hat as she spread the afghan over his daughter, tucking it snug around her. "How does the snowgirl story work out? Does she live happily ever after at the north pole?"

"Yes." Macie sniffled. "Her daddy turns into a snowman so she's not alone."

"Sounds like a fantastic story to me." Chelsea's

smile could light up the darkness. "I'll see you around, Macie."

"See ya around."

"Thanks." He cleared his throat, but the gruffness remained. The woman's kindness touched him and drove some of the ice from his heart, on this of all days, the three-year anniversary of his wife's death. "The blankets. I'll need to return them."

"I live at the end of Wild Rose Lane. It says McKaslin on the mailbox. You can't miss it." Her gentleness vanished when she turned to him, crossing her arms over her chest like a shield.

Yeah, he'd made a good impression, all right.

"I'll be praying for Macie, that her arm is all right." Chelsea McKaslin stalked away, her boots squeaking in the snow.

Before he could answer, the thick veils closed around her, the shadows claimed her. She was lost to him and he was alone in the storm.

Chapter Two

What a gorgeous morning. Chelsea breathed in the crisp, icy fresh air, stomped the snow off her boots and tromped through the backyard of her family's property. She blinked against the sun's bright glare and glanced over her shoulder at the horse barn. For as far as she could see, white fields rolled and preened beneath a pale blue sky. Wow, it was good to be back for keeps.

The frigid air burned her lungs as she trudged toward the door. Slow going through the accumulation, but much easier since the blizzard had stopped. Last night's trek home had been interesting. Drifting snow made it impossible to drive, so she'd pulled over on Wild Rose Lane and walked a half mile. She'd nearly turned into a snowman, too—well, a snow-woman. Thinking of Macie, Chelsea smiled to herself as she clomped up the porch steps.

"Ha! I saw you coming." The door swung open and Meg, her younger sister by four years, crooked one slim brow. "What are you doing up at this hour? You got in so late. You should be sleeping in. Taking advantage of your time off."

"What can I say? I needed a horse fix."

"I totally get it." Meg braced one slim shoulder against the open door, model-gorgeous with her lean looks, beautiful face and long brown hair. "Good news. The county snowplow just finished clearing the road."

"Yay. Now I can rescue my car." Her eighteen-year-old Toyota might not be snazzy, but she'd gotten attached to it over the years. She'd inherited it from Mom when she'd gone off to college. She tromped through the doorway and into the warm house. "Do you know what I really need?"

"I'm afraid to ask."

"Someone to give me a lift."

"Sorry, I can't pick you up." Mischief twinkled in Meg's brown eyes before she disappeared into the kitchen. "But I can give you a ride."

"Really? Isn't it a little early in the morning for puns?"

"Sorry, couldn't help myself. Sara Beth is rummaging around in the basement. Thought I should warn you."

"Okay." Chelsea shouldered the door shut. Sara Beth was sister number two in the McKaslin lineup, Chelsea's younger sister by two years. "I guess the real question is what she's looking for?"

"House lights. We're putting them up today." Meg's voice echoed from the kitchen, leaving a lot unsaid. This would be the first Christmas they would be stringing up the lights without Mom.

Chelsea swallowed against a tide of emotion and plopped down on the nearby bench. She could do this. She could face this Christmas without Mom. "Are you going to hang the dangly icicle ones or the multicolor ones?"

"Not my call. The person who puts up the lights gets to decide." A *clink* sounded from the kitchen. "I can tell you, it won't be me. Remember what happened when I was on a ladder last?"

"Was that when you got stuck on the roof?"

"Putting up the big star, per Mom's directions, remember? And it totally wasn't my fault the stupid ladder decided to fall over. I haven't trusted one since."

"You think the rest of us should?"

"Sure, as long as it isn't me." A clunk of a stoneware mug being set on the granite counter punctuated her humor. "I strung the lights the last time with Dad, if you remember. Sara Beth said she's not partial to ladders, and Johanna is at the vet clinic working with Dad and who knows when they will be back, so that only leaves—"

"Me." Great. She wasn't fond of ladders either. She tugged off her boots. This is what she got for being the oldest and out of town when her sisters were planning Christmas. "Why don't we wait for Dad?"

"Because I think it will be too tough on him to have to do it."

"Right." Because he'd always put them up for Mom. Boy, this Christmas wasn't going to be easy. She unzipped her barn coat and hung it in the closet. "Guess it's my turn, then."

"I knew you'd do it. I kinda think it's best to surprise Dad with the decorations, you know, like a new tradition. Now it's our turn to put up the lights for him."

"I like it." She followed her sister's voice into the kitchen. Bayly, one of their two dogs, opened an eye to watch her enter the room, let his lids fall shut and went back to snoozing on his bed near the family room's crackling fireplace. "But before I do anything, I've got to fetch my car and I have a few things to do in town."

"What things?" Meg set a teacup on the breakfast bar. The scents of cinnamon and spices wafted upward on the steam.

"Go to the bank. Hit the bookstore. Check up on a few people."

"What people?" Meg's eyes narrowed curiously.

That was the problem having so many sisters. No privacy. Plus, sisters tended to be nosy.

Maybe she was missing Seattle after all. She cozied up to the breakfast bar and plopped onto a swivel chair. "I came across a little girl and her dad in the cemetery last night. She fell off the curb in the storm and broke her wrist."

"Poor little one." Meg set a second cup on the counter. "So, tell me. Handsome dad?"

"I didn't notice."

"How could you not notice? Honestly." Meg shook her head with disapproval. "Any chance he was a single dad? I keep praying for you to find a really great guy."

"He was a widower. That was why he was at the cemetery."

"Oh." Meg circled around the kitchen island and took the neighboring chair. "How sad for them."

"Yeah," she agreed, sipping her tea, remembering Macie. And the father…Dr. Kramer. She ought to really dislike him, she hadn't appreciated the way he'd manhandled her, suspecting the worst when she'd only been helping his daughter, the child he'd let wander away from him. But then, it only took a moment of inattention and if he'd been at his deceased wife's grave…her heart twinged with sympathy. Sympathy was one thing, but remembering the way snow had settled on his broad shoulders was entirely another.

"You're praying for me to find someone? Really?" She sipped her tea, which warmed her instantly. "Even though you know I have a five-year plan?"

"You and your plans." Meg leaned back, legs crossed. "Don't tell me. You made a pro-con list, too."

"Don't mock my pro-con lists. I wouldn't be able to make a good, workable plan without them."

"I wasn't mocking, honest. Just curious. Where are you putting romance in your plans?"

"I'm not." When the time came, she had a very definite idea about the kind of man she would fall for—dependable, honest, loyal and kind— and even then, he would have to fit into her plans. Wasn't that what plans were for? "Am I smart, or what?"

"How exactly do you want me to answer that?"

"I'm not sure I do." Chelsea rolled her eyes, shaking her head. Somewhere outside rang a dog's distant bark.

The doorbell chimed, echoing through the sprawling house. Bayly lifted his head from his dog bed, gave a halfhearted bark and yawned wide. His watchdog abilities were sorely lacking.

"Ooh, could be the delivery dude." Meg bounded from her chair, mug in hand. "Maybe my package finally came. No, stay where you are. You'd better rest up while you can because in about ten minutes, you have a ladder to climb."

"Will I be climbing it alone?" She arched one brow, kind of wondering what else her sister had planned for her.

"It depends." Meg's voice trailed behind her as she wove through the house. "If it's not a busy day at the clinic, then Johanna will be able to lend a hand."

"Probably not busy in this weather." Their dad ran a veterinary clinic, now joined by Meg and Johanna, who were vets, too.

"Hey, that's not the delivery truck." Meg's surprise lilted through the house. The door whispered open, but Chelsea's feet were already on the floor of their own accord. She pushed away from the breakfast bar, driven by the tingle at the back of her neck.

"I'm Michael Kramer." A man's rich baritone rumbled from the doorway. "Is Chelsea home?"

"Sure. Let me guess. You're the cemetery guy." Meg tugged the door wider. "Here she is right now. Howdy, sis. There's someone here to see you."

"So I heard." She did her best not to gape at the tall, solemn and handsome man towering in the doorway. Make that *remarkably* handsome, now that she got a good look at him in the full light of day. He wore a black wool coat, jeans and hiking boots. She'd be hard-pressed to recall when she'd last been around such a good-looking guy.

Wow, Meg mouthed.

It was hard to argue. Wow, indeed. His chiseled face, lean lines and wide, dependable shoulders made her heart catch. Her knees went weak and her heart skipped two beats, but it had to be from the surprise of seeing him again. A perfectly understandable reaction.

"Chelsea." A hint of a smile shaped the corners of his chiseled mouth. The intensity of his gaze zeroed in on her like a target. "Looks like I got the right house."

"G-guess so," she stuttered out. Great. Brilliant. She'd never been what you'd call confident around handsome men. "I'm surprised you're out and about on these roads."

"They've been plowed. I wanted to return these." He held up the afghans her mom had made. "Thanks again."

"Not a problem." Somehow she was in front of him and multicolored granny squares tumbled into her arms. The yarn, soft and full of memories, smelled of fabric softener, clearly freshly laundered. That was thoughtful of him. Wasn't it? "How is Macie?"

"Better. She's talking with your sister." He gestured down the walkway, pointing out of sight. At least, she *thought* they were out of sight. Maybe she couldn't see Sara Beth or Macie because she couldn't make her gaze move past the man.

He loomed above her at well over six feet, his sandy-brown hair tousled by the wind. *Blink, Chelsea,* she told herself. *Stop staring.*

"It was a simple fracture, no complications, no real swelling, so the doc casted her last night." His voice dipped, tender with fatherly concern. "She's much better this morning."

"Glad to hear it." Chelsea dumped the afghans unceremoniously on the nearby bench, wishing her gray matter would kick into gear. Why couldn't she be amusing and charming and unaffected? Where was her confidence when she needed it?

Footsteps thumping up the porch steps saved her from fruitlessly searching for something clever to say.

"Hi, Chelsea!" Macie peered around her dad. Daisy, the McKaslins' yellow lab, hopped up and down with excitement at her side. "Sara Beth said I can choose the lights."

"She did, did she?" Now that her vision had cleared, Chelsea spotted her sister down the walkway, leaning against one of two ladders.

"Sorry." Tall, sweet and beautiful, Sara Beth gave her lustrous brown hair a toss. "I couldn't resist letting her pick."

"I totally get it." It was so easy to remember she'd been little and the four of them rallied around

Dad shouting out their preferences for lights. Once, he'd put up two different strings, one over the top of the other, just to keep everyone happy. The house had been so brightly festive, you could see the Christmas lights a good half mile across the horse pasture. She blinked away the recollection of Mom's laughter at the sight. "Which ones did you like best, Macie?"

"The white ones." Her round face was relaxed and smiling, a welcome change from last night. "I like those the best because they're like icicles."

"Me, too. Good choice." Chelsea grabbed her winter coat off the tree by the door and shrugged into it, crossing the porch. "Hey, I like your pink cast."

"Me, too."

"And it matches your coat." Aware of Michael's gaze prickling across her back, she knelt to get a good look at the girl's arm. "You were brave to get an X-ray and see a doctor."

"I didn't have to go the hospital. Dad took me to his office." Macie gulped, wrestling with her emotions. "The hospital is where my mom died."

"Mine, too." She shared an understanding look with the girl. "Do you know what you need?"

"What?" Macie's forehead crinkled.

"Stickers. I don't know how to tell you this, but you can't go around with a cast like that. It's just plain wrong."

"It is?"

"Sure. You've got to decorate it." Chelsea felt the tug of Michael's gaze, drawing her to him. There went her heart rate, galloping again. "Why don't you two come in?"

"I think we could spare the time." The deep notes of his voice shivered over her, as warm as steaming cocoa on a cold winter's day. "But you're clearly busy."

"Nothing that can't wait. We're talking about stickers here. Important stuff."

Suddenly Meg had returned—Chelsea wasn't even sure where she'd went. Meg, ever helpful, grinned exceptionally brightly from the hallway. "Come in, Macie. Let's go raid my sister's stash of stickers, okay?"

"Okay. Does she have a good stash?" Macie trailed into the house and down the hall. Daisy— Dee for short—scrabbled after her, doggy nails tapping a cheerful rhythm on the wood floor.

Alone with Michael, Chelsea took a deep breath, fighting the unsettling sensation of being close to him. It troubled her, trickling in like the cold wind through her coat and she shivered. Now what did she say? Nothing brilliant came to mind. Funny, she'd been uncomfortable with him last night for an entirely different reason.

He looked as uneasy as she felt. He jammed his fists into his coat pockets, looking like a male model striking a pose for winter wear. He shifted his weight from his left foot to his right and his high intelligent forehead furrowed as if he were searching for something sociable to say to break the lengthening silence.

Talk about awkward. He was still standing on the porch! Why hadn't her brain worked enough to invite him in? "Maybe you'd like some hot chocolate?"

"No, I don't like hot chocolate." His deep blue eyes transmitted his apology.

"Okay, then—"

Like an answer to a prayer, Sara Beth breezed up the steps, her face pink from the freezing wind. "Hey, Chels, it's time to get the lights up. We've got two hours tops before Dad rolls in."

"Right." The perfect excuse. "Maybe you could take Michael inside? Maybe get him something to drink."

"Sure. Hi, Michael." Sara Beth nodded, apparently acquainted with the man. A total surprise. "Come on in and make yourself at home. Maybe keep an eye on Macie. No telling what kind of trouble she and Meg will get into with those stickers."

"Stickers are not my domain. I'd rather avoid it." Another hint of a smile tugged at the corners of his mouth. "Besides, when a man sees a ladder, he has to climb it."

"Fine by me." Sara Beth shot Chelsea a grin and wagged her eyebrows. "I'll just go and fetch the lights. You two can get to work."

"Us two?" Chelsea shot her sister a death-ray glare. What was going on? "Wait, Sara Beth. Aren't you going to help?"

"Why should I, when we have a volunteer to do it?" Sara Beth sashayed down the hallway, leaving Chelsea alone with the man again.

Why did she suspect her sister had some kind of motive?

"I know Sara Beth from the riding stables." He broke the silence, taking the first step in the direction of the ladders. "She's teaching riding. She's Macie's instructor."

"That explains it." Chelsea closed the door behind her, shivering in the cold wind on the porch. "Sara Beth is the best."

"So I hear. Macie wants to be like her."

"Good call. Sara Beth is awesome. She's a world-ranked rider." Pride for her sister came through. "She won a bronze medal in the last Olympics."

"And a gold and a silver in a couple World Championships. I know all about it." Not because he knew anything about the McKaslin family, but because a little sprite he knew talked on and on about it.

"How long has Macie been riding?"

"Since the school year started." His attempt to make her life as normal as possible after her mother's passing. Not an easy thing to do, and remembering how hard it had been for Macie still choked him up. "My wife loved horses. For our last Christmas together, Diana promised riding lessons and a horse to Macie. I will never forget our last holiday together as a family."

"Those memories are great treasures. That was like Mom's last Christmas with us. We did everything to the max, decorating, gifts, the food. All that mattered was that she was with us."

"I understand." His throat tightened. As he ambled down the shoveled pathway, his feelings stirred. Maybe it was the bracing air that burned in his lungs with each breath or the quiet beauty of the December morning. "I would give everything I have to give Macie one more day with her mother."

"I know the feeling, wanting to do anything to turn back time." Her understanding touched him like a blessing. A gentle gust of wind caressed her light chestnut locks, which fell like gleaming silk over her slender shoulders. "I have to believe that love lives on."

"Me, too." He wasn't sure what was happening to his stoic heart. He tipped back his head to study the placement of the ladders, stretching up two stories. Footsteps crunched close behind him and Sara Beth waltzed around the corner of the garage carrying a big plastic storage tub in both arms. It looked like an awfully awkward bin, so he headed toward her. "Let me get that."

"*I'll* get it." Chelsea sailed in front of him, and the long lean line she made as she plunged through the snow made him think of music videos and wholesome country stars and the innocent grace of Christmas carols. Her long hair swept behind her like a rippling melody. She handled the big tub with ease. "Sara Beth, you're staying to help, right?"

"Sorry, I changed my mind." Sara Beth's dark eyes looked him up and down, and her grin was just shy of mischievous. She turned on her heel and tossed over her shoulder, "I've got better things to do."

"Someone is getting coal in their stocking come Christmas morning. I'm not naming any names, but it could be you." Chelsea flipped off the container's lid and sunlight shone on the thousand miniature lights inside. "Can you believe it? She abandoned me."

"What's the world coming to, right?"

"Right." Her brows arched, an adorable little twist of her beautiful face, and exactly how lovely she was hit him like a snowball to the chest. Her porcelain jawline and dainty chin gave her a sweetheart's look. Her sloping nose and friendly blue eyes could make stronger men than he stop in their tracks. She didn't seem aware of it as she plucked a coil of white lights from the container. "You don't look like the handyman type. So, really, why are you doing this?"

"Because one good turn deserves another." He took possession of the coil, lifting it from her slender fingers. "Besides, it'll give me practice. Macie is bound to talk me into stringing lights at home, and this way I'll make all my mistakes here."

"With our lights? Right." She wasn't fooled. She fished out a plastic bag of gutter hooks, sneaking another peek at him. Had he always been so tall? He had to be a few inches over six foot and he smelled good, like pine.

He snagged the plastic bag of gutter clips and seized a ladder rung. Without a second of hesitation, he climbed with confidence and speed. Since she didn't want to be shown up by a man, she headed for the second ladder, took a steadying breath and grabbed hold of a metal rung. *Lord, please don't let me crash to my death.*

Determined not to visualize doom, she launched off the ground. The ladder trembled and shook with every step she took.

That didn't bode well, but she kept her eyes on the next rung and didn't look down. Maybe the height wouldn't bother her if she didn't see it. Made sense, right?

The wind gusted, wobbling the ladder. Eek. She clutched the metal, although there was no crashing to the ground and no doom. Still, she hated the way the ground seemed miles away. She swallowed hard, determined to keep going.

"Why don't you get down?" Michael's deep baritone warmed the words, he really was a good guy. "I've got this."

"You aren't getting rid of me that easily. Sorry." She might not like heights, but no way was she quitting. Not when she'd made up her mind to do something.

Determined, she trained her gaze on the gutter above. Three steps more. Two. Safely at the top she slowly uncoiled the string of lights and hoped Michael didn't notice how much her hands were shaking.

Chapter Three

Michael nudged the small plastic hanger into place, tried to keep his attention on the eight or so inches of white stuff piled precariously on the roof over his head and failed. His gaze slid to the woman clutching the gutter lip with what appeared to be all her strength. Why didn't she just let him do this? "Are you always this stubborn?"

"Usually more." If she gripped the gutter any tighter, something was going to break. "Rumor has it, stubborn is my middle name."

"Hey, mine too." His own laughter surprised him, causing him to almost lose his balance. The ladder wobbled, his hand shot out, hit the snow on the roof and a cold avalanche rained over him. Icy stuff hit him in the face, slid down his coat collar and kept coming in a glittery white fall, blinding him. He probably looked like an idiot.

"Good one," she quipped. "Now who has a death grip on the gutter?"

"I'm usually more suave than this. Smooth. Debonair." He batted snow out of his face.

"I noticed that the first instant we met." Humor laced her words.

She had to remind him of that, didn't she? Not that he could see her just now because another wave of falling snow smacked him in the face.

"Need any help?" she asked.

"No." Debonair he was not. He blinked snow out of his eyes. "This looked easier from the ground."

"It always does."

The avalanche finally stopped and he ran a gloved hand over his eyes, able to blink. Ice clung to his lashes and gleamed in the sun so when he looked at her, she seemed framed by light, surreal, a vision come to life.

"Maybe it would have been smarter to let the sun melt some of this before we started, but did I think of it? No." She clipped her string of lights into the plastic hook. "My sisters wanted to get the lights up before Dad gets home."

"So he's usually on light duty?"

"True, but one of us always helps him. The job goes faster that way and besides, you can't help wanting to spend time with Dad."

"So this time you want to surprise him?" He

cringed when a trickle of ice slipped between his shirt and his collarbone.

"Something like that. See, Dad always put up the lights with Mom's supervision. Since she's been gone…" There were no words to describe the loss. She focused on stringing the lights, getting them to sit just right in the clips. "Mom was big into Christmas. Lights and decorations and Christmas carols playing. The works."

"You don't want your father to feel her loss while he's hanging the lights." Understanding softened his granite features and warmed the low notes of his voice. "It's easier to go on when you don't stop to feel the loss."

"Exactly." Interesting that they had this in common. She didn't like that her estimation of him crept up a notch. "Is that what you do? You try not to feel the grief?"

"I try to forget it. Bury it. Psychologists might not agree, but it works for me."

"Me, too. Last Christmas we couldn't put up as much as a tree." She thought of the seasonal cheer, the festive joy, the touches of caring her mother had brought to the holiday and to her family. "This year, we're trying to do Christmas the way she would have wanted."

"It's a tough thing to do. Two Christmases have gone by for us, this will be our third." He hung another length of lights. "It was hardest on Macie."

"I'm so sorry for that. Do you have other family in the area?"

"My folks live in town. They moved here after I set up practice, to be closer to their granddaughter." The wind gusted, ruffling his sandy brown hair. "Mom always does Christmas right, and she can cook. Can't wait for her turkey and stuffing."

"My mom was a good cook, too. But me? Not so much." She clipped more lights in place, ignoring the fact that her fingertips were numb with cold.

"You? A bad cook? I don't believe that. You look like there's nothing you do badly."

She would *not* be charmed by his compliment and a hint of a dimple. "I'm too clinical. I approach cooking like a lab experiment. Exact measurements with the potential of anything going wrong."

"But the outcome is edible."

"Mostly, but it's been frozen dinners for years. Med school, intern, resident. No time."

"I remember well." His gaze met hers, zooming across the distance between them as if there were no distance, as if they were no longer strangers, as if he were way too close.

Shyness swept through her and she jerked her gaze away. Her forearm bumped the gutter and snow tumbled onto her head, momentarily blinding her.

"Don't worry." His words carried on the wind. "Eventually the ice melts and then you're just wet."

"Something to look forward to." The snow just kept on coming. She sputtered, held onto the gutter for dear life and thought she heard the rattle of a ladder that sounded suspiciously closer than it used to be. Sure enough, the avalanche stopped and there was Michael so near she could reach out and push him.

"At least the lights look good." He leaned across the foot and half of space between them to brush snow from her face.

Air stalled in her throat, choking her. Really, she could do it herself, but she didn't move. She blinked, able to see the shaven texture of his strong, square jaw and flecks of ice blue in his irises.

"Are you okay?" Concern crinkled pleasantly in the corners of those irresistible eyes.

"Sure. That was invigorating."

"Nothing like a snowy winter's morning on the roof." His glove swiped snow away from her coat collar.

That was really nice of him, but he was making her dizzy. Somehow she managed to draw in air. "Thanks, but I'm not Macie."

"Right, got it." He handily grabbed the end of her lights dangling from the clip and plugged his string in. The icicle lights dangled and glowed, lovely even in the daylight. "I just didn't want you falling."

"I appreciate that." She cleared her throat, surprised that her words came out a little strained. "Falling would be a bad thing for many reasons. Just think, if I landed in the rosebushes, they'd never be the same."

A dog's happy bark rang like a bell from beneath the porch, scattering sparrows away from the bird feeder. Dee pranced down the steps and down the walkway, head held high, tongue lolling, as excited as if she were leading a parade down Main Street. Macie followed with a few telltale cookie crumbs on her coat, flanked by Sara Beth. Meg shut the front door and trailed down the porch steps after them.

Finally, her sisters had come to rescue her. Not that hanging around with Michael Kramer had been so terrible. No, she certainly couldn't say that. "Looks like your daughter has come looking for you."

"So I see. I guess that's my cue to leave, unless you want me to stay and help."

"Oh no, I have plenty of help, if I can motivate my sisters, and you have a daughter to take care of." She gripped the top rung and moved carefully down one step and the next. "Plus, I'm anxious to see what she's done to her cast. Let me see, Macie."

"It's all Christmassy now." The girl held her arm up for all to see. "They had lots of stickers, Dad. It was awesome."

"But in the end we went with an animal and Christmas theme," Sara Beth explained, folding a lock of straight dark hair behind her slim shoulder. "Doesn't it look stunning?"

"I think the color scheme works," Meg added, her dark eyes twinkling.

"Do you like it, Dad?" Macie beamed, her pink cast artfully decorated with candy cane stickers, white snowflakes and gold stars, Christmas trees and cats and dogs. "And I got to pet Burt."

"Who's Burt?" he asked.

"Burt liked that, I'm sure." Chelsea leaned in to check out the stickers. Her light chestnut hair tumbled across her face, shielding her as she admired Macie's sticker choices. "Now that's one fantastic cast."

"I know," she said in her high, sweet voice. "Burt is a cat, Dad. You know, what I'm asking for Christmas."

"I'm well aware." No secret there. He caught hold of his child's shoulder, nudging her toward the car.

"I was going to ask for a white kitty, but now I want a gray striped one like Burt." Macie crunched through the snow with her pink boots.

That was already on his Christmas to-do list.

Find a kitten for Macie. Not that he knew where to find kittens. The pet store? Ads in the paper?

The Lab gave a cheerful bark and loped ahead, glancing over her shoulder to smile at them in her doggy way.

"And I want one that hugs me," Macie reminded him for the fiftieth time.

"I know." He yanked open the SUV's passenger door. "I'm still planning on giving you a stocking full of coal. No presents at all."

"Oh, Daddy." Macie rolled her eyes, not believing him. He couldn't imagine why.

He swung her up onto the seat. "Time to go, little one. You're looking a little pale around the gills."

"Fish have gills. Not me."

"Sure you do." He helped her buckle up, aware of the women standing nearby, especially one woman, although he couldn't explain it. He didn't have to turn around to picture her standing ankle deep in snow in her navy coat and with her wavy chestnut hair dancing in the wind.

"Thank you for the stickers," Macie called over his shoulder.

"You let me know if you need more. We have plenty," Sara Beth answered, although it wasn't her that he noticed as he turned to close the door.

"The icicle lights look the best. You were right, Macie." Chelsea gestured toward the house where two strings of lights flashed in the glancing sunlight. "Thanks for the help, Michael. It's more than my own sisters would do."

"Hey, I could have done it," Sara Beth corrected good-naturedly.

"But I just didn't want to," Meg confessed with a smile.

"This is what I get for being the oldest. It's a burden." Chelsea rolled her eyes, feigning displeasure, but her smile gave her away.

Had he ever seen a day so bright? He couldn't remember one. The light blue sky shone vivid against snowy clouds sailing by in speeding puffs. The gleam and glitter of sunshine on the miles of snow stole his breath. And Chelsea shone the brightest of all, making him notice.

Two vehicles rolled into sight, cresting the roll of Wyoming prairie.

"It's Dad," she announced and bit her bottom lip.

"Early." Meg shook her head.

"And the lights aren't finished." Sara Beth sighed. "Oh, well. It was a good thought."

"It was." Chelsea waved to her father behind the steering wheel. The chains on his pickup chinked as he rumbled around Michael's SUV in the driveway and pulled up in front of the garage. A familiar beige vehicle lumbered into view. "Hey, there's my car."

"Rescued by another sister?" Michael asked as he opened his door.

"Yes, no idea what I'd do without Johanna." She waved to the youngest of the McKaslin sisters. Johanna waved back, her neon blue mittens flashing behind the glare of the windshield before she pulled into the garage.

"I hope the rest of the light hanging goes well." He folded his six-foot-plus frame into the front seat, his door thudded shut and the engine purred to life. His window rolled down. "I'll see you around, Chelsea McKaslin."

Whether that was a threat or a promise, she couldn't tell.

The SUV motored away as Macie waved with her good hand, and Dee barked and whined, perhaps disappointed she wasn't the one going for a ride.

"He was totally good-looking," Meg commented. "An eleven on a scale of ten."

"Was he? You know me. I'm not looking." Although she couldn't explain why she watched Michael's SUV rumble down the road and out of sight. It didn't mean she was interested in him. No way. "I have a no-man plan, remember?"

"I thought it was a five-year plan." Sara Beth just had to point that out, didn't she?

"A five-year plan, a no-man plan. Same difference." She forced her gaze away from the swell in the prairie that had swallowed Michael's SUV from her sight and turned on her heel, concentrating on the one man she could count on. "Dad."

Dee spotted him and barked, leaping to race to his side and pant up at him adoringly.

"Hey, girls." Grant McKaslin patted the Lab on her head. "I see you're putting up the house lights. Looks good."

His words sounded strained. Emotion gleamed in his eyes.

"Love the lights!" Johanna bounded out of the garage as the door lowered behind her. "Time for lunch, but, Chelsea, I'll pitch in after we eat. I can't wait to see them all lit up."

"Your mom would be pleased." Dad said the words they were all thinking. He held out one arm to draw Johanna close, the other to pull in Meg. "Let's get in and warm up. Chelsea, we found your car at the side of the road."

"Thanks for bringing her in."

"No problem. I hope you girls have soup on the stove. I'm frozen clean through."

Dee raced ahead, tail wagging, leading the way to the front door. Chelsea glanced over her shoulder to catch a last look at the half-finished lights dangling from the roofline. If only Mom were here, she thought, full of longing, but that was not to be. With a sigh, she tapped up the porch steps behind her sisters. As Dad held the door open for them, a gust of wind chased her inside and stirred the icicle lights above as if with a loving hand.

Michael tucked the fleece throw gently around his sleeping daughter while the TV hummed with a kid's movie in the background. Clouds had moved in to dim the sun shining through the living room window, hinting at more snow on the way.

Macie sighed in her sleep, snuggling against her pillow pet. Her brown hair tumbled over her forehead, framing her face. Such a sweet girl. He pressed a kiss to her cheek, backed away from the couch and padded across the carpet, careful not to wake her.

The house phone rang. He caught it on the third electronic jingle, lifting the cordless receiver out of its cradle. He recognized the name on the electronic display. "Hey, Steve."

"Hey." His colleague sounded chipper. "I'm about to head out with my wife, but I wanted to check on your girl. How's her arm?"

"Doing as well as can be expected. She's napping now." He tucked the receiver against his shoulder and eyed the lunch dishes in the sink. "What are you doing checking up on patients? You just can't take a weekend off, can you?"

"I'm trying. We're going snowmobiling. We're just about to head out."

"Sounds fun, so what are you doing on the phone with me?" He opened the dishwasher.

"Fine, so I'm not cutting back on my workload like I planned." Steve didn't sound guilty about that, not at all. "Eventually I'll have to, since the new doctor I hired to help me starts on Monday."

"I had no idea. Last I heard you were going to wait until January to start looking for someone." He turned on the faucet and ran a lunch plate through the stream.

"I've had my eye on this doctor for a while, she's available and the timing is right." Steve's smile warmed his words. "One of these days I won't have to come into the office at all. The rest of you are so good, I'll be absolutely unnecessary."

"You? No chance of that." Steve Swift was one of the most knowledgeable doctors around. "No one can fill your shoes."

"I don't believe it for a second." Steven chuckled and it was good to hear him sounding happy. "My wife is calling. Better go."

"Have fun. No more thinking about work. You're not on call, remember?" He slipped a plate into the dishwasher rack, trying to imagine the unathletic man on a snowmobile. "And no accidents, got it?"

"Got it. No worries, Laura has done this before. We're going on a tour up in the mountains. Great, now she's honking. I really do have to go."

"Have fun, Steve." He set the phone on the counter, shaking his head. Seeing Steve broadening his horizons was gonna be very interesting. Maybe because although twenty years separated them, they were very alike. Workaholics dedicated to their profession, men of science and men who didn't have room for much else in their lives.

What about the new doctor? And why hadn't Steve said more before this? Why the mystery? Then again, that had been the plan since his health scare. He'd had a minor heart attack, but it had been a wake-up call for Steve. *Less time at work,* he'd said in the break room one day. *More time spent living life to the fullest.*

Couldn't argue with that. The light clink of the dishes as he loaded the dishwasher kept him company in the lonely room. In Michael's opinion, this was living life to the fullest. He had a job he loved, a comfortable home and a daughter to care for. Speaking of which, he grabbed the phone, dialed his mom and waited for the phone to connect. He swished the soup pan through the water, fit it into the bottom rack and closed the dishwasher door as she answered, sounding breathless.

"Am I catching you at a bad time?" He reached for the paper towel roll.

"No, just came in from running errands. It's cold out there!" June Kramer blew out a breath for emphasis and something in the background rustled. "The grocery store was crazy. Everyone stocking up for the next storm. They say it's going to be a doozy. How's my granddaughter?"

"Napping." He peeked around the corner. Yep, still asleep.

"Good, she needs rest to heal. Say, I bought cookie makings. Figured she might want to help me with my first batch of Christmas cookies. That ought to be a proper excuse to spend time with her. How does tomorrow sound?"

"I'm sure she'll like it." He was thankful to the Lord that his mom was the kind of grandmother who would step in and fill the void in Macie's life. His mom was gold in a hundred different ways. "Why don't you take her home after church? I'll pack a bag if you want to keep her overnight."

"Yes, yes, yes! Oh, you've just made me a very happy grammy." More rustling bags and the sound of a refrigerator opening. "I'm glad I bought the supplies for her favorite supper."

"You were already planning, admit it." He grabbed a paper towel and a spray bottle of eco-friendly cleaner. "That I suggested you keep her worked into your master plan."

"It did. Your dad will take her to school come Monday, as long as it's not a snow day. Then, again, maybe we'll keep her forever."

"Sure, go ahead and try." He squirted the length of counter and wiped it down. "In the meantime, I need your help with one of Macie's Christmas gifts."

"Do you mean *the* Christmas gift, the only one she wants?"

"The kitten." No idea how that was going to work out, and he was a little afraid to think about it. "Where do I find one? I want a good one. The right one."

He had no idea how to know which one would be the right one. Surely all kittens were nice, but how did he find the one that would be the loving friend Macie wanted?

"I have no idea. I know, not what you wanted to hear. But I have my sources. Let me make a few calls and talk to some friends. I'll get back to you."

"Mom, you're fantastic."

"Don't I know it," she agreed happily.

Relieved, he turned the conversation to what was going on in his parents' lives. He listened while he wiped down the table and started sorting clothes in the laundry room. Wind gusted against the side of the house, and the last of the sunlight bled from the sky. He said goodbye to his mom and lit a fire in the fireplace. By the time the new storm's first snowflakes fell, the Kramer house felt warm and snug. This was as good as life got, he thought, watching his daughter sleep. He couldn't ask for anything more.

Chapter Four

The weekend flew by. Chelsea barely had time to breathe settling in at home—unpacking her car, putting up the rest of the lights and then there was church on Sunday. Monday morning blew in with a fresh accumulation of snow and a storm that sent snow drifting over roads and made the mile drive into town challenging. She pulled into the little parking lot behind Dr. Swift's medical clinic ten minutes late. Totally hating being late, she shoved open her door, hauled her bag from the passenger seat, slipped on a sheet of ice and landed on her bottom.

Great. Just great. Cold seeped through her wool slacks as she levered back onto her feet, grabbed her keys and prayed Dr. Swift wouldn't be too unhappy with her. He'd been clear. Staff meeting starts at seven-thirty. Halfway to the door she noticed a reflection in a glass window. Her headlights. Double great. With a sigh, she tromped back through the snow. Hurry, hurry, hurry. This was no way to start her first day of work for the man she'd looked up to all her life. Steve Swift was not only her new boss but her longtime mentor. He'd encouraged her in her studies and he'd been there for their family when Mom had fallen ill—

Her right foot slipped, she went down on her knees in the same ice patch she'd fallen in earlier. Fabulous. So, maybe she was missing Seattle's rain just a little. She pulled herself up holding on to the door handle, unlocked her car, turned off the lights and trekked back through the snow. Really, the day had to get better from here, right?

Her cell chimed the moment she set foot through the back door. Warmth enfolded her, chasing away the chill as she fished her phone out of her bag. A text message stared up at her.

Hope your first day goes well, sweetheart, her father had written. I know you'll do great.

That was her dad, always there for her.

Thanks. She hit Send, smiling as she unwound her scarf, imagining him at work at the vet clinic, cradling a cup of coffee and carrying on a conversation with any animals who happened to be in the kennels.

She unwrapped her scarf and her phone chimed again. Not Dad this time.

Praying UR first day is fabulous! Johanna's words

marched across her screen cheerfully. Meg says U go, girl!

Okay, this was the upside of sisterhood. Maybe being back in Wyoming wasn't so bad. She unbuttoned her coat, shrugged out of it and tapped out an answer. So far I haven't broken a leg. Have a great day, 2. Dinner tonight?

At Jeff's Diner, Johanna answered. Six o'clock. UR treat.

MY treat? She texted back.

Becuz U love me and because I'm broke.

Hard to argue with that. She'd missed her sisters living so far away. Weather aside, it really was good to be back.

The door swung open without warning. Snow blew in like a blizzard, borne on a strong gust. A tall man dressed in black shouldered in, his silhouette strangely familiar. A dark knit hat hid his sandy-brown hair and for a moment the snow shielded his face, but she knew him even before he rammed the door shut.

Michael Kramer. *Doctor* Michael Kramer.

"What are you doing here?" she asked before her brain kicked in. "Wait, don't answer that. Let me guess. You work here."

"Guilty." He tugged off his hat. He smelled like snow and pine. Very Christmassy. Very nice. "My name is on the stationery, at least it was the last time I checked. Are you here to see one of the other doctors?"

"See one? No, I work here. I'm the new—"

"Pediatrician." He blinked in surprise, his gray matter suddenly stuck in neutral. Why hadn't he guessed it? Maybe because when he'd first met Chelsea McKaslin, he'd had his daughter's broken arm on his mind. The second time he'd met her, it had taken most of his mental acuity not to dwell on how beautiful she was. "Right. Guess I should have known."

"So, you didn't read the memo?" Blue eyes sparkled up at him, bright with humor.

Yeah, he deserved it. "I'm focused, I admit it. I'd rather practice medicine than the business of medicine."

"I hear you there." She swiped a lock of light chestnut hair out of her eyes. Melting snow clung to her like a tiara, twinkling in the light. "Steve hired me last month."

"That explains it." He led the way down the narrow hall, flipped on a bank of lights and clipped into the break room. No scent of coffee met him. The machine was dark, the lights off. Looked like everyone was running late this morning due to the worsening storm. "I'm just here two days a week. I'm in Jackson the other three. Must have missed the official announcement."

"Working here has always been my plan since I

was a kid." She seemed at home as she plopped her bag on the edge of the central table and fished out a plastic lunch container. "Steve must be running late?"

"Late? No, he—" He shook his head, realizing he was watching her sweep over to the refrigerator like she'd caught his eyes with a tractor beam. Stop looking, Michael. He yanked open a closet door and shrugged off his snowy coat. "Something tells me you didn't hear the news."

"No." She plopped her lunch on a rack and closed the fridge door. Concern gentled her eyes so blue they were almost lilac. "What about news?"

"Steve went snowmobiling on Saturday and had a run-in with a tree." Why couldn't he stop looking at her?

"Uh-oh, that's never good." She waltzed toward him, slipping out of her winter coat. Her slim eyebrows knit together, her heart-shaped face wreathing with the same tender caring as when she'd been helping injured Macie at the cemetery. "Is he okay?"

"Other than a broken femur, sure."

"He broke his leg?" Her eyebrows shot up, her jaw dropped open. "Oh, no, is he looking at surgery?"

"Apparently it's not indicated, but you know the saying, doctors make the worst patients. Steve might not be telling the whole truth. He left a message on my phone last night." He jammed his coat on a hanger and rammed it onto the rod. A faint knock brought him up short. Sounded like someone at the front door. "I'll check it out. What are the chances it's him and he forgot his keys?"

"High, I'd say." That would be just like the tough, seasoned doctor to come to work when he should be on bed rest. Alone in the room, she slipped her coat around a hanger and hung it up. The silence gave her a moment to digest new developments. So, she'd be working with Michael. Awesome.

Her phone chimed again. When she checked the screen, she smiled at Sara Beth's message. I know you'll work 2 hard today. Don't forget to take a little time and enjoy the moment. U R a doctor now, Chels. Just like you've always dreamed.

Yes, it was a dream, she thought, checking out the coffeemaker. It was prepped and ready to go, so she hit the switch. As it gurgled to life, spitting and popping, she shrugged on her white coat and took a moment to savor the feeling. She'd accomplished one goal—getting here—and now it was time to work toward another, which was being the best doctor she knew how to be.

"Dr. McKaslin?" Michael's voice rang down the hall. He held open the waiting room door for someone, his face a professional, granite mask. Obviously in doctor mode. "We have a patient.

Could you take a look at her? Her regular doctor, Dr. Benedict, isn't in yet."

Goody. Trying not to do a Snoopy dance, Chelsea plunged her hands into her coat pockets and said in her most doctorlike voice to the woman stooped over in the doorway, "I'll be happy to help you."

"The snowblower broke, so I had to shovel our driveway," the young mother explained, stooped over. Snow clung to her blond curly hair and a toddler clutched her right hand. "Bad idea. My back seized up and look at me. I'm bent over like a capital *C*. I was on my way to the hospital but the last thing I want to do is wait in the emergency room with Lily, since it's flu season. Then I saw your lights on. You have no idea how grateful I am."

"Glad we can help." Chelsea shoved open the door to the first examining room she came to. "Come on in and let's see what's going on."

"Bless you." Mom and adorable tot ambled into the room.

Probably a muscle spasm, Chelsea reasoned, but she'd need X-rays to be sure there was no disk injury. She turned to Michael, but he was already gone, pacing down the corridor toward the front office with his shoulders braced and spine straight, likely to fetch the patient's file. She couldn't explain why she was even watching him. There was something about the man's effect on her she didn't entirely like.

"You were such a brave girl." After a long day of doctoring, Chelsea held the bowl of Tootsie Pops for Alicia Wigginsworth so she could pick a flavor. Tootsie Pops were a tradition for Dr. Swift's little patients, and now for hers. "Grape is my favorite, too."

Alicia nodded in shy agreement before burying her face in her mother's shoulder.

"Thanks, Dr. McKaslin." Mrs. Wigginsworth patted her child's back comfortingly. "Tell Dr. Swift I'm praying for a speedy recovery."

"I will." She opened the examining room door, chart in hand. "The injection site may be a little sore for a few days. If her fever doesn't start heading down, call. You know the drill."

"I do. I'll let you know if there are any problems," the mom promised as she stepped into the hallway.

"Goodbye, Alicia." She waved at her patient, who watched her with tear-filled eyes over her mom's shoulder. It wasn't easy being little, or being the one who had to give a shot, but in a few days' time the sweet little girl should be feeling a whole lot better.

The after-hours corridor echoed as the door to the waiting room whispered shut. The vague, muffled conversation between Mrs. Wigginsworth and Audra at the front desk were the loudest sounds in the echoing hallway.

"Looks like you made it through your first day unscathed." Dr. Susan Benedict emerged from the break room, slipping into her winter coat. She was a young doctor, a few years out of residency, tall and slender with lovely long ebony curls. "Congratulations. Especially considering it was one of those days. Everyone tripped, fell, shoveled too much, caught a bug or slid off the road."

"No kidding. I was so busy, I didn't realize I'd missed lunch until a few hours ago. Crazy, but I loved it." She rolled her stethoscope and slipped it back into the pocket of her white coat. "That was clever of Steve to run the staff meeting off the computer."

"Praise the Lord for video chat. It's going to be interesting to see how long Steve can hold out and not come into the office." Susan's amber eyes twinkled as she tugged warm gloves out of her coat pockets. "Thanks for seeing my patient this morning. Word is that Lenore is home, icing and heating just like you ordered. The muscle relaxant seems to be helping."

"Good to hear. You're heading out?"

"While I can. That's one thing you've got to learn straight off. When the coast is clear, run for it or the phone will ring, someone will knock on the door or something will happen and you'll be stuck here for another hour." Susan offered a warm smile. "It's a great profession, but it can take over everything if you aren't careful. And since the coast is clear, I'm heading out. I'll see you tomorrow, Chelsea."

"Have a lovely evening." She headed down the hall toward her office, smiling. She wasn't alone in the clinic. Audra was still finishing up in front and a few doctors were finishing up their chart work. Michael was one of them, his office door firmly shut against intrusion.

She hadn't exchanged another word with him through the day. She'd been so focused on her work and so had he. It was just as well because that's where her attention needed to be. With a sigh, she waltzed into her office, small and impersonal, with just a desk, a computer and a phone. A small window looked out on the back lot where her car was covered by a foot of snow.

Her pocket chimed, the sound kick-starting a part of her brain that had gone dormant. Her sisters! Dinner. Yikes! What time was it? No clock in her office, so she hauled out her phone. Her eyes zeroed in at the time on the screen. Six-twelve. She was twelve minutes late!

Where R U? Meg's text stared up at her accusingly. We're waiting.

I'm coming! She tapped in, hit Send and fished

a pen out of her coat pocket. She scribbled a note on Alicia's chart, rushed down the hallway and slid the chart across the back counter in the receptionist's direction. "Thanks, I gotta go."

"Have a nice evening." Audra shoved a lock of auburn hair out of her eyes. "Careful. The last few patients said it's really icy out there."

"Thanks for the heads-up." She dashed into the break room, grabbed her uneaten lunch from the fridge, her bag from the shelf and shrugged into her coat. A few wraps of her scarf so it was snug around her neck and she was out the door.

One foot slid out from under her, but since she still had hold of the doorknob, she had something to hold on to. She managed to stay upright, but Audra hadn't been kidding!

Slow down, Chelsea, she told herself, something Mom used to say. As she picked her way across the dangerously slick parking lot, she could hear her mother's voice in memory. *Chelsea McKaslin, slow down. You'll always get where you're meant to be. God will make sure of it, so stop rushing.*

She missed Mom's advice, even if she hadn't always agreed with it. She brushed falling snow off her cheek, wishing she could turn back time so she could see her mom again and hear those words in person.

A few more steps brought her to her buried car. Wait, correct that. Her *seriously* buried car.

It would take time and effort to dig out the poor thing. This was a total disaster. She hated being late! Grumbling to herself, she dug her phone out of her pocket. Her thick winter gloves didn't make it easy to type out a message.

Car under tons of snow. Order without me. She hit Send and her phone chirped sadly. It wasn't able to get a strong enough signal to send in the thickly falling snow.

Great. She jammed her phone into her bag, studying the monstrous white lump her car had become. Where to start? And with what? The little ice scraper under the front seat wasn't up to this job.

"Looks like you have a problem." A smoky baritone broke through the snowfall.

"Michael." Impossible to see him through the storm's thick white veil. Wait—there he was. A hint of muscled shoulders, a shadow in the downfall and she ordered her pulse to stay calm. "Are you always one of the first here and the last to leave?"

"Depends on the day." He broke out of the storm, swathed in black and dotted with snow. "Do you need help?"

"Nope, I can get it." She'd learned a long time ago to be wary of dudes offering "help." Wasn't that how she'd met Nick? Another total disaster. "I'm just figuring out my best strategy."

"That would be getting four-wheel drive."

"No kidding, but I'm partial to my old Toyota." In more ways than one.

"Hey, it was a suggestion."

"A good one *if* my school loans weren't kicking in."

"I hear you." He hit his remote and his door locks popped. He leaned in and started the engine, leaving it to idle. "Hold on, there's no way you're getting out of this lot with that car. The snow is deeper than your bumper."

"I was just pondering that particular dilemma. There are so many, I'm not sure where to start." She rubbed snow from the driver's side window with her glove and peered inside. Her poor car. "What are the chances the plow people are coming?"

"Not my area. Audra would know. She's in charge of calling them, but it looks like they forgot the back lot. Again." He knocked snow off his back door and opened up. "Remind Audra in the morning. That's your best bet."

"So, in other words, just leave my car here?"

"It's locked up and with this storm, it'll be safe. Not too many car thieves out." He produced a long-handled ice scraper from the back of his four-wheel drive. "I can give you a ride."

"Maybe I'll walk." The diner was, what, a mile

away? Okay, maybe not. "Better yet, I'll give my sisters a call. One of them will pick me up."

"So, are you still in denial about being stubborn?" He tackled the side windows with his scraper. Snow rained to the ground.

"Me? Nope, I've never noticed." Denial was the best way to go.

"Yeah, right. You and me, both." He opened the passenger door for her. "Climb in while I clear."

"I'm not sure I feel comfortable with that."

"You're one of those difficult women, are you?" A faint smile cracked the line of his mouth.

"Difficult? No, but I'm not sure about you, Dr. Kramer." She plopped her bag on the floor in front of the passenger seat. "You hardly said a word to anyone all day. I didn't notice it, anyway."

"I get what's going on here." He circled to the windshield and raked twelve inches of snow off the glass. "You've heard what everyone says."

"No, but now I really want to know what everyone says."

"I'm focused at work." He tried to pretend none of what he'd overheard mattered. Cold. Heart of stone. Glaciers had more personality. "I don't hang out in the break room making friends with my colleagues."

"You hung out in the break room with me, but I'm not sure I'd feel comfortable calling you a friend."

"Me either." It wasn't easy ignoring the dazzle

of her blue eyes, sparkling with a hint of humor. "There's nothing friendly going on here."

"Glad you agree."

"It would ruin my reputation. I've worked hard for it." He pulverized a chunk of ice on the windshield with the edge of the scraper.

"So, in other words, don't friend you on Facebook?"

"At least don't tell anyone if you do." He freed the windshield wipers from the ice on the glass and strode to her side of the vehicle. "Would you get in? You're letting all the hot air out."

"Do you know what I think?" She squinted at him, her amused gaze roving over his face, really looking. "I noticed everyone at work seems intimidated by you, but you're not so bad."

"I'm not so good." Not socially anyway, although it wasn't for a lack of trying. There was a time when he'd once tried hard to fit in, to take down the walls that had always surrounded him. "Where am I taking you? Home?"

"No, to Jeff's Diner." She hopped on the seat, reaching for the belt. "Thanks for saving my sisters from having to come get me."

"At least I'm good for something," he quipped, closed her door and trudged through the deep accumulation. His boots squeaked, the ice beneath the snow threatened to send him sprawling and there went his vision again, strangely arrowing to the gorgeous brunette in his vehicle.

"Don't let this get around." He dropped into his seat, kicking snow off his boots. "My reputation at work will be ruined."

"That might not be up to me." She gestured through the frosty windshield toward the faint shadow as the wind gusted, giving a smudged glimpse of the building's back door. "Audra's waving. Looks like your reputation is doomed."

"No way." He yanked off his gloves and buckled in. Heat zoomed out of the vents, clearing a tiny spot in the glass. "Foggy windows. What are the chances she can see you?"

"Saved by a technicality."

"I'll take what I can get." With all four wheels engaged, he gave it a little gas, spun the wheel and lumbered across the lot.

Chapter Five

"I noticed your name on the letterhead," she said before silence could fall between them. "I didn't know you were a pediatric oncologist."

"That's me." He rubbed off the fog on the windshield with his shirtsleeve and maneuvered around the building, hitting a patch of ice, which thankfully garnered all of his attention. All day long, she'd been there at the back of his mind, a thought here and there. He wondered how she was doing, wondered why it was so easy to talk to her. Why did he feel comfortable with her? Why her?

"That has to be difficult dealing with critically ill children every day." Understanding so tender in her voice tempted him to open up.

Opening up was the last thing he wanted to do. Nothing good could come from it. But did that stop him? No. He turned out of the lot, keeping an eye on traffic, and down went his reserve.

"It's not easy, but it's what I'm called to do." He couldn't look at her, it would be too personal, so he focused on the icy road barely visible through the pounding white flakes. "When I was eight, I lost my little brother, Danny to leukemia."

"I'm so sorry. That had to be so hard to go through."

"There was nothing I could do to help him. Nothing I could do to make him better or stop him from dying." He paused, as if unable to say more.

"I know how that feels." Her confession hovered in the air between them, too personal, too vulnerable. "I so do. When you'd do or give anything to save a loved one, but it's impossible."

"Exactly. I remember standing beside his hospital bed and vowing to be a doctor when I grew up. That way I could help other kids' little brothers." He shrugged self-consciously. "Here I am, thirty years later."

"Helping critically ill children and their families." New respect curled through her, warm and powerful. "I've had to diagnose cancer a few times during my residency. Telling a loving parent that their child has a terminal illness was one of the hardest things I've ever had to do. Dealing with it every day, doesn't that get you down?"

"I look at it another way. I help them fight for life." He hit his blinker and pulled to the curb.

"There is nothing more important than fighting for life so love can go on."

"I know what you mean." She thought of her mother's loving words she would never hear, all Mom's phone calls and emails, her listening ear, her caring heart and the hugs she would never get again. Through the snowfall she spotted the diner's striped awning. No doubt her sisters were seated behind one of those windows watching her. "Thanks for the ride."

"No problem." His gaze found hers, his cool-blue eyes warm with emotion. "I've got Macie waiting."

"Right. Didn't mean to stare." She rescued her bag from the floor. "Is her arm still hurting?"

"It's better. She spent Sunday night at my parents'. My mom likes to spoil her." He tore his gaze from hers, staring hard at the snow tumbling down on the windshield in a dizzying swirl. "With the snow day today, I almost hate to think what I'll be walking in on. Girl time. It makes a man uncomfortable."

"Right. It's tough being a dude."

"That's the truth." A small smile touched the corners of his mouth, his dimples threatening to show. "Hair bows, French braids, movies about unicorns and rainbows."

"My father survived it. I'm guessing you can, too." She unclicked her seat belt, but the thing she couldn't undo was the warmth of connection settling between them. The size of the passenger compartment seemed to shrink, the air felt too thick to breathe. A zing of electricity battered her heart. Okay, that was totally weird. Her comfort level shot into an unfamiliar zone. Suddenly, he felt too close, she was too aware that this guy's handsomeness exceeded all others and really, now that she noticed, he was making her palms damp.

Alarm bells went off in her head. Go. Run. Escape. She grappled with the door handle, tumbled out into the snow and hoped she at least appeared dignified. "Well, have a safe trek home. Tell Macie hi."

"I will." A muscle tensed along his strong, square jaw. He didn't exactly look at her, more at the snow falling directly over her right shoulder. "Have a good evening."

"You, too." Heart strumming, she closed the door, stepped back on the icy sidewalk and her boot slid on a patch of ice. She overcorrected, her hand swung into the air and instead of looking like a klutz, maybe, just maybe, if Michael happened to glance in his rearview mirror she might come off as giving a breezy wave. That way she wouldn't look like the shaken, confused woman she was.

Whatever had happened between them just now, she never wanted it to happen again.

The wind gusted, rousing her. Time to hunt

down the rest of the McKaslin girls. The tap of snowflakes on the sidewalk kept time as she crossed the icy concrete, opened the diner door and nearly bumped into the owner, carrying a tub of rock salt.

"Hey, your sisters are already here." Jeff held the door for her as she tripped by. "I saw you slip. Are you okay?"

"Just peachy." Great. If he noticed, had Michael? Not even wanting to know, she marched passed him, unwinding her scarf and spotting her sisters immediately. Mainly because Johanna was leaning out into the aisle, waving.

"Hey, you made it." Johanna patted the seat beside her and scooted over against the window. "You didn't answer my text."

"We worried," Sara Beth chimed in on the other side of the table. "Then I saw Michael's Lexus pull up and I thought, yay."

"Why yay? You know this means my car is stuck." And let's not even think about what Sara Beth might really mean. "Totally stuck. I couldn't have driven out of the lot with my oil pan intact. Maybe even the muffler."

"Diversion isn't going to work with us." Meg, tucked next to Sara Beth, toyed with the straw in her chocolate milkshake. "Twice now you've spent quality time with the handsome doctor."

"You two seem to really get along." Johanna waggled her brows.

"Sure, what do you want me to do? Be rude to him? I can, if you want me to." Honestly. Just because her heartbeat felt thready, didn't mean the man affected her. Okay, fine, to be honest, he really did. But she didn't have to admit it, she didn't have to acknowledge it. Maybe it would be smart to ignore it. It might go away. "I work with him, right? And why didn't anyone bother to tell me he shared an office with Dr. Swift?"

"Uh, because I didn't know." Johanna didn't look sorry about it. "Did you know, Meg?"

"No, as I'd never met the man before."

"I knew, but I figured you already knew. I mean, you've spent so much time talking with the man." Sara Beth's dark eyes flashed with amusement. "But I won't tease you about it, if you don't want me to."

"Thank you. I would appreciate that." Because if they stopped talking about him, then maybe she could get Michael out of her mind—the man and his reason for becoming an oncologist, the man and his heart-arresting half smile— Oops. She was doing it again.

"Are you ready to order?" the waitress interrupted.

Perfect timing. A change of mental focus was

exactly what she needed. No more thoughts of Michael Kramer.

"Cheeseburger, curly fries and a chocolate shake," she said without looking at the menu. So much for her healthy diet. Recent events called for heavy artillery, meaning French fries and chocolate.

"The same." Sara Beth handed over her menu.

As Meg and Johanna ordered, Chelsea wondered how Michael was doing on the drive home. The roads looked terrible. She didn't know why she cared so much, but that was the problem. A big one. Huge. Massive. Detrimental.

"So, any ideas on what to get Dad for Christmas?" Johanna gathered her steaming teacup in both hands.

"Dad? He's impossible to shop for." Meg flicked a long lock of dark hair over her slender shoulder.

"He has everything and wants nothing." Sara Beth gave a thoughtful look. "There has to be something we can get him. Something he doesn't even know he wants."

"No idea what that would be." Johanna scrunched up her forehead in thought. "Nope, no idea."

"Then we'll just have to mull." Chelsea wished she had an idea for the perfect gift, but right now all her gray matter could think of was the one man she shouldn't. "An answer will come to us."

"It should be something really great. He deserves that." Sara Beth's eyes shone with emotion.

"He does," they all agreed together in unison and fell silent, leaving so much unsaid. Loss, love, the wish for the kind of Christmas Mom would have wanted.

The waitress returned with their cheeseburgers. The clatter of dishes, the smell of hot fries and the waitress's friendliness broke the silence between them. After making sure they didn't need anything else, she hurried away to help other customers.

"My turn to say grace," Johanna spoke up, catching hold of Chelsea's hand. "Lord, thank you for bringing us together safely again, in good health and with hope in our hearts. Please watch over our dad, because we worry about him being lonely, and take care of our mom, wherever she is in heaven with You. Let her know how much we love her. Amen."

"Amen." The word slipped past Chelsea's dry throat. She really did miss Mom.

"So, Chels, are you coming with me to choir practice?" Johanna grabbed the ketchup bottle propped up against the napkin dispenser and squirted a puddle onto her plate.

"I didn't know there was choir practice." She tore off the paper wrapper on her straw.

"Weren't you paying attention in church?" Meg

took the ketchup bottle from Johanna. "Practice for the candlelight service starts today."

"You always used to sing in it when you were home." Johanna dove into her fries.

"That was when I was in high school." It was kind of weird to be home again, living in her old bedroom while so much had changed. Nothing stayed the same. "I don't know how my work hours are going to go, so I can't commit. Probably I'll be working late a lot of weeknights."

"You didn't work late today," Sara Beth pointed out. "Besides, we're all going and since you need a ride, you'll have to come with us."

"Not that I'm objecting, but you could have told me that before." Honestly. She plunged her straw into her milkshake and took a sip. Sweet, cool, chocolatey. Can't go wrong with that. "I guess I *could* join and see how it goes."

"Ah, she fell into our trap." Johanna waggled her brows and bit into another fry. "Success?"

"Success," Meg and Sara Beth agreed in unison.

Her sisters. What would she do without them? "Pass me the ketchup, and let's be clear. I have responsibilities. My obligations at the clinic come first."

"Right."

"Absolutely."

"Understandable."

All three sisters smirked at her, as if they had other plans.

Yes, it was definitely good to be home again. *Lord, thank You for my sisters,* she prayed.

"Michael!" His mother swept open the front door of her home, squinting out into the dark swirling storm. "I was just starting to worry about you. You could have called."

"I needed both hands on the wheel. Bad roads." He stomped snow off his boots and marched into the warmth of the house. Cold to his bone marrow, he unzipped his winter coat but kept it on and peeled off his gloves, heading straight for the hearth. The crackling heat drew him like a tractor beam, offering comfort, kind of the same way Chelsea McKaslin's presence did, and that more than troubled him. He'd never noticed anyone the way he noticed her. And considering how easily he'd opened up to her, well, that bothered him. Big-time.

"Daddy!" Macie bounced up from the coffee table, where she'd been kneeling, clutching a bright red ball ornament. "Look what we're doing. Me and Gramps picked out the tree and me and Grammy are decorating it."

"Looks like you're doing a good job, too." He knelt down, awkward, folding the little girl into his arms. He'd never been the nurturing parent.

He'd always left that to Diana, who'd been so good at it. How he hated that he was inadequate for the job left to him. He moved away, ruffling her soft dark hair. "Glad you're helping Grammy with her tree. Saves me from being recruited."

"Don't think that will stop me," his mom kidded with a wink.

"Good thing you only live a block away." Jay, his father, lumbered through the house, snow sticking to his wool shirt and his thinning hair, a load of wood in one arm. He must have come in through the back. "The weathermen say we're in for a hard blow."

"That's not what I wanted to hear." Last year's relatively mild winter was only a dream at this point. Two storms in three days. Who knew what the rest of the month held? "I'll have a tough trip into Jackson tomorrow. Smells like you've got dinner in the oven, Mom. I'll pack up Macie's things and we'll get out of your way."

"You'll do no such thing." June Kramer was never one to let her granddaughter go easily. "Michael, take off your coat and stay awhile. I made your favorite chicken dish. Oops, that's the oven timer. You fill in for me and help Macie decorate the tree."

"Me? I don't have an artistic eye. Not even an artistic cornea."

"Excuses won't help you, son." His father nodded toward the television in the corner, set on mute, where a new announcement scrolled across the bottom of the screen. "I've learned a lesson being married all these years. Never go against the woman of the house."

"Hey!" June called from the kitchen. "I heard that, although it is the truth."

"See how rough my life is?" Dad quipped.

"There are worse things." Michael took a few pieces of wood from his dad and knelt down, fitting them into the grate. "Ebola, for instance."

"Or the black plague," his dad quipped back, filling the wood box beside the hearth. "You're right. That does put it in perspective."

"Glad to help." He and Diana had never had the kind of harmonious connection his parents did. The fire's heat fanned his face, thawing him out, but nothing could stop his mind from boomeranging back to Chelsea. They did have a natural accord. Troubling. Very troubling.

"Dad, look." His daughter gestured toward a delicate glass ball hanging from a branch. "Hmm, maybe it'd look a lot better over here."

Macie hung her ornament thoughtfully on a low branch of the fresh-smelling fir towering between the couch and the front window. She stepped back, dark curls framing her round face, and considered her work. With a serious nod, she seemed satisfied. "Much better."

"You're doing a good job, kiddo." He wrestled another red glass ball out of its plastic holder and handed it to her.

"I know." She pursed her lips together, debating where it should go. "Hey, Dad, do you know what?"

"What?"

"Did you know you could get a sleigh ride? They have 'em at the riding stable." She took the ornament from him and hung it carefully. "It's really cool. Lots of other girls get to go on a ride with their dads. I thought we could go, just you and me."

"I'll think about it."

"Promise?"

"Promise." Sleigh riding. Not sure how he felt about that. He dug another ornament out of the box, Macie took it and wandered around to the far side of the tree. Where did his mind go? Not staying focused on his family. Not on worrying how he'd get all the way into Jackson tomorrow, nearly an hour's drive in good weather. Not even on his child. Chelsea McKaslin. She filled his thoughts like presents in a stocking. He couldn't forget the sight of her bounding down from his Lexus with the snow dancing around her, her movements graceful, always moving as if she heard an inner song.

The faint scent of strawberries and vanilla clung

to his coat as he shrugged it off. His stomach felt fisted up, troubled by something he did not want to feel. Chelsea McKaslin was a colleague and a fellow doctor, that was all. Nothing more. And that was the way he was going to start thinking of her.

Problem solved.

"Too bad choir practice was cancelled," Chelsea quipped from the backseat of Meg's SUV. "That's it. It's official. I'm not meant to sing in the candlelight service. It's a sign from above."

"Nope, sorry, you're wrong." Johanna shifted in the front passenger seat. "It's not a sign. It's more like a delay."

"I'd already texted the choir director, so you're committed." Meg took her eyes briefly off the snowy road to grin at Chelsea in the rearview mirror. "She was totally thrilled, as they're short on altos."

"Ever since Mom passed," Johanna explained. "It feels right, doesn't it? It's like Chelsea is taking her place."

"It's fitting." Meg nodded, keeping her eyes on the road this time, since a wind gust battered the side of the vehicle. "Mom would have liked it."

"Remember how she sang right up until the last few months?" Johanna's voice turned soft, full of love. "Her last Christmas service, remember how we had to wrap her up so well because of the cold?"

"It was ten degrees." Chelsea remembered flying in on Christmas Eve for a fast trip home and how frail Mom had looked. They all knew she was losing her battle, even then. "I stepped out of the airport into that cold air. It cut like a razor straight through my clothes. There you were waiting for me at the curb. I can still see Mom smiling and waving. Her dark curls, caring eyes, a smile as bright as dreams. I should have taken a leave from school."

"No, she wanted you to finish your residency." Meg chanced another glance in the rearview, her dark eyes serious. "She said you were right where you were meant to be."

"I know, she told me." Over and over, but that hadn't stopped the guilt or the sense of duty that warred with Mom's wishes. Chelsea had always been ambitious, but what was ambition in light of a family member's illness? Nothing, that's what. "No one knows how many times I almost walked away from school. From everything I'd ever worked for."

"I know." Johanna twisted in her seat, her lovely face wrinkled with regret. "I had to leave her, too. I was in my last year of vet school, remember?"

"Don't feel guilty, Chels." Meg slowed for a barely visible curve in the road. "You have no idea how much hope you gave Mom. She told me so. She used to say all the time, that life goes on. It encouraged her to know that we were all going to be okay."

"Seattle was too far away." She watched the white flakes beat at the windshield, feeling the vastness of the dark. Headlights reflected back on the falling snow, keeping the road ahead a mystery and unseen—just like life. You could only do the best you could and trust the Lord to lead the way. But that didn't stop the sense she'd somehow failed Mom. "Phone calls and emails weren't enough."

"Are you kidding? She called you every day." Meg's forehead crinkled, her eyes soft with understanding. "Trust me, it was enough. Besides, she'd like you taking her place in the choir. It's like a full circle thing, you know?"

"I know." Chelsea sat back in her seat, spying a faint flash of light through the storm. The flicker grew brighter as Meg maneuvered through the deep snow. The shining icicle lights came into view, marching along the roofline of home.

"Mom used to love those lights," Meg said to no one in particular as she hit the garage remote, unnecessary since everyone already knew it. It was impossible to see the lights and not think of Mom.

The headlights from Sara Beth's truck bobbed into view behind them—she'd swung by the vet clinic to pick up Dad who'd stayed late. It was good Dad was home, too. Chelsea grabbed her bag, hopped off the seat and the garage echoed around her. It felt good to know they were all safe and out of the storm. She was thankful for that.

Chapter Six

The week whizzed by at an alarming rate. The snow stopped falling, the sunshine came out, but the temperatures weren't high enough to melt the accumulation. Chelsea took a second to glance out the window after another crazy-busy morning at the clinic. The Wyoming landscape lay still and frozen. Sunshine glanced off white, sparkling snow like Christmas morning.

"I looked over the charts you left on my desk." Dr. Steve Swift's friendly tenor broke into her thoughts. His crutches clunked on the tile as he hobbled closer. "Good job. Couldn't have done better myself."

"There wasn't much to it. Lots of colds and flu, and a few cases of strep. Everything's routine." With her tablet computer tucked in one arm, Chelsea pushed away from the break room window, greeting her mentor with a smile. "How is your first day back at work?"

"Going about as well as my wife predicted it would." A pleasantly stocky man of average height, Steve crutched farther into the room. His warm personality made everyone feel at ease with him, and his round face wore a perpetual smile. "My leg is throbbing. Time to head home and put it up, lay back and take it easy."

"You? Take it easy? I don't believe it." Chelsea fetched a plastic container from the fridge and snapped it open. Lunchtime. The scent of Sara Beth's chicken salad made her mouth water. It was fabulous to have a sister who really knew how to cook. "Have you ever taken it easy a day in your life?"

"Hey, I'm turning over a new leaf. Becoming a more laid-back man." Steve's green eyes sparkled with good humor. "It's the new me."

"Really?" She plopped her lunch on the table next to the window. "You couldn't stay away five whole days."

"It was an administrative thing. I had to come in and sign checks."

"Right, because no one could have dropped them by your house." So not fooled, Chelsea poked a straw into her juice box.

"I didn't want either Audra or Carol to go to all

that trouble. Besides, who would cover the front desk and the phones?" Steve lumbered over to the other side of the table and stared out the window. "I'm just trying to be thoughtful."

"Admit it. You couldn't stay away." She sank into a chair.

"Just between you and me? Yeah, I miss this place. It's been a madhouse this morning. Just the way I like it."

"Me, too." At least she was getting lunch today. That was an improvement over other days earlier in the week. "I've totally enjoyed covering your patients."

"With you and Susan doing such a good job, not a single patient is gonna miss me." Steve shrugged, shook his head and turned from the window. "There's the wife. She told me I'd better not keep her waiting, so I've got to go. She has a schedule to keep. She's knee-deep in projects at the church."

"It's a busy time of year there. How is she managing to do everything and take care of you?"

"It's a mystery." Steve crutched toward the door. "Keep emailing me daily reports, call if you have a patient question and above all, keep up the good work."

"Thanks, Steve. You take care of that fracture."

"Count on it." With another rattle of his crutches, he trudged through the door and out of sight.

Did it feel good to get off her feet? Absolutely. She relaxed into the cushioned chair back, closed her eyes and bowed her head for a quick grace. That done, she turned on her tablet computer and pulled up her day's to-do list. Shockingly long.

"Sorry to bother you, but we've had three more walk-ins." Audra from the front desk knocked on the open door. "Can you help cover them? Please?" She pleaded with clasped hands.

"How can I say no to that? Give me ten minutes." Chelsea excelled in speed-eating. Plus, that would also give her enough time to add a few dire items to her to-do list.

"Terrific." Audra smiled in relief. "Oops, looks like you have company."

"I do?" One glance confirmed it. She spotted a very familiar figure standing in the doorway. "Johanna, who let you back here?"

"I bribed that nice lady in front with these." She held up a small bakery box and flipped the lid. "I was running errands for Dad—"

"At the bakery?" Her apple for dessert, sitting nice and red and polished in her lunch box, didn't look nearly as tantalizing as frosted Christmas cookies.

"No, I was walking out of the bank and spied the bakery across the street. A cookie craving hit and I thought, why fight it?" She plunked the box on the table and plopped into a chair. "You didn't answer my text."

"From this morning? No, because I didn't read it."

"Really? How could you resist reading a text from me? Usually they're riveting." Johanna selected a cookie and bit into it.

"I was busy treating a four-year-old with strep at the time. This is my first break all morning." Sandwich first, then cookie, she told herself and gathered up half of her sandwich. "Although I've been dying of anticipation wondering what your text said."

"You should be. It involves a certain handsome doctor."

"What handsome doctor? Here in this clinic?" That stumped her, or at least she pretended it did. "You mean Steve?"

"No. Steve? Sure he's friendly, but he's old enough to be our dad." Johanna opened her purse and tugged out a cheerful red envelope. "No, I'm talking about someone else, and don't think I don't know what you're doing."

"What am I doing?"

"Denial. I've been there. I've done it, too. When I didn't want to admit I was falling for Roger Wiggenbottom in tenth grade." Johanna bit into her cookie. It really looked tasty.

"I'm not in denial. Of course I know you're talking about Michael Kramer. I'm pretending you aren't." She wished she'd nearly forgotten the man. She hadn't seen him since Monday. "You can't go reading anything into that ride he gave me. My car was stuck."

"Right, I understand completely." Johanna waved her cookie around as she talked. "Denial. Sometimes you need it. Otherwise, how would we cope? Dudes are trouble, let's face it. They make you fall in love with them, they make you vulnerable and the next thing you know, they break your heart. Denial is the smart way to go."

"Is it still denial if you aren't interested in the man?" Honestly, Johanna couldn't be more wrong. Chelsea took a bite of sandwich, shaking her head. "Why are you here again?"

"I was in the drugstore getting Christmas cards for the vet clinic's patients when I spotted these." She set down her cookie to open the envelope. Colorful stickers spilled out, Christmassy ones with glitter and foil, depicting a dozen little kittens, each with red bows. "I took one look and thought, Macie."

"Definitely." Hard not to think about that darling little girl. "They'd go with her cast nicely."

"Awesome. Then these are for her. I'll replenish my sticker collection later." Johanna shoved the envelope across the table and zeroed in on the computer. "Hey, what are you doing?"

"My to-do list, what else?" Chelsea shrugged and took another bite of her sandwich.

"Right, when it comes to you, what else indeed?" Johanna leaned over and stole the tablet with a flick of her wrist. "Most people use their iPads for things like watching movies, playing games. You know, for having fun?"

"Hey, that's mine!" Chelsea protested.

"Do you even know what fun is?" Johanna quirked one eyebrow turning her attention to the screen. "Double check labs, follow up calls to yesterday's patients, update charts. Just what I suspected. This is all about work."

"Because it's my work to-do list." She took a sip of juice. "What do you expect?"

"It's *work,* Chels." Johanna admonished her with her big, gentle eyes. "Nothing but work."

"Hey, I have other lists." She chomped down another bite of chicken salad. "They aren't all about work. There's my church list, my reading list, my home chore list."

"Boring." Johanna laughed and tapped the screen. "Let's take a look, shall we? There's got to be something less dull in here."

"There's my healthy eating list. That's a rollicking read."

"Hey, what's this?" Johanna's eyes widened as she studied the screen, tipping it so that Chelsea couldn't see what she was reading. "Now this is interesting."

"What did you find? My Christmas shopping list?"

"No, something *much* better." Johanna squared her shoulders, cleared her throat and started to read. "The perfect man wish list—"

"No! Don't read it. That's not really on there, is it?" She dropped her sandwich and made a grab for the tablet.

Johanna kept it deftly out of reach. "Number one, kind. Number two, doesn't think of himself all the time—"

"Give it back." Chelsea lunged across the table, heat flaming her face. "That isn't meant for just anyone to read."

"Am I just anyone?" Johanna's wide-eyed innocence didn't fool anyone, but she did hand over the iPad. "I'm your dear sister you should be sharing stuff with. So, this is interesting. A list for a man. Should I be surprised? No. You have lists for everything."

"Hmm. I may have to make a pro-con list for keeping you for a sister." Chelsea shook her head, settled back in her seat and glanced at the screen. Her list from a long-ago day stared up at her, bringing with it a not insignificant wince of pain. "I'd forgotten that list was on there. It must have been in the folder of stuff I transferred from my main computer when I got this thing."

"I'm kind of curious, if you want to talk about it. I didn't know it was painful. I'm sorry."

"Hey, don't be. It's not painful." Not anymore. Okay, maybe it still was, but not much. "I—"

A knock at the door interrupted.

"Ten minutes," Audra announced apologetically. "Sorry, but a new walk-in is bleeding. Not bad, but still."

"Looks like I gotta go." Perfect excuse not to think about her perfect guy wish list. She turned off the tablet, tucked it into her arm and gathered up her lunch things. "Patients to see, wounds to stitch."

"Have fun. And don't forget a cookie." Johanna held out her bakery box, Chelsea took one—how could she resist? The sweet sugary treat melted on her tongue. Divine.

"And thanks for the stickers." She plunked the remains of her lunch in the fridge and came back for the red envelope. "I'll leave this on Dr. Kramer's desk."

"Dr. Kramer? Not Michael?" Johanna bounded out of the chair. "Wait, I get it. It's denial. So, see ya later. Meg and I are gonna try to get Dad out of the clinic on time."

"Good, because I worry about him. He works too much."

"Like someone else I know." Johanna sailed through the door with a finger wave, her boots whispering in the hallway as she made her way to the front.

"I don't work too much," Chelsea said to herself. She liked responsibility and being the one to get things done. What was wrong with that?

Nothing. Not one thing. She munched on her cookie, heading toward her office where she deposited her iPad, grabbed a few files and distributed them on her way to the exam rooms. Two folders for Susan's desk, one for Dr. Steve's and after knocking and getting no answer, she breezed into Michael Kramer's office, left the red envelope on his desk and sailed back out, closing the door behind her.

"Your next patient is in exam three." Audra met her with a relieved look. "The nurse is taking info, but we've seen this kid before. He's one of Dr. Swift's."

"Right." Straightening her white coat, Chelsea went for the hand sanitizer and stepped into the examining room, not surprised to see a mischievous-looking boy, probably around five or six, with his hand wrapped in a dish towel.

"Sledding accident," his worried and harried mother explained. Clearly this kid was a handful.

"We've had a lot of those lately," Chelsea assured her, kneeling down to take a look.

* * *

"Dr. Mike?" Seven-year-old Howie Lansing looked up from his hospital bed. Even washed-out from a long surgery and surrounded by beeping monitors which were necessary in ICU, he managed to look like trouble waiting to happen.

"What is it, buddy?" He clicked his pen, chart notations made.

"Can I go home yet?" Big gray eyes pleaded up at him. His mother, seated beside him, leaned closer to caress his head soothingly. His fine blond hair crackled with static electricity.

"Not yet, but I'll be the first to tell you when. You're a good, brave boy." He nodded to Mrs. Lansing, who was pale with exhaustion and worry. "Nora, you have my number. Call if you need anything and, Howie, you nailed the surgery. No patient I've ever had has done better."

"I know." Howie settled into his pillows, his left arm wired, pinned and in traction.

Michael gave thanks for the procedure that had allowed the surgeon to remove the cancerous bone and save the arm and the boy's life. "Don't forget to get some rest, too, Nora. Where did your husband go?"

"To fetch me some lunch." Nora Lansing's face bore the stress and worry that came from having a critically ill child. "I just couldn't eat earlier."

"Make sure you take care of yourself, too.

Howie needs you to stay healthy." He offered what he hoped was an encouraging smile, winked at the boy and headed out of the unit. Checking his tablet computer in the hallway, he studied the to-do list his nurse had compiled for him. Looked like it was time to head to the office for his two o'clock appointment, which was little Kelsey Koffman.

It was going to be a tough one. He hauled out his cell as he wound his way through the hospital and punched in a call while he rode the elevator. Mrs. Koffman answered on the eighth ring, out of breath, as if she'd run to catch the phone.

"How's Kelsey today?" He headed straight through the parking garage to his SUV. "I know she has a two o'clock, but I wanted to make sure she's up to the trip into town."

"She's pretty weak." Kate Koffman sounded matter-of-fact. She could have been discussing the weather. The way parents held themselves together in a crisis varied, but their commitment to their children rarely did. "I've been up all night with her."

"How's her discomfort level?" He clicked his remote and opened the door.

"It doesn't seem worse, at least that's one good thing." Kate paused, as if holding back emotion. "She's afraid the cancer is back. She can't sleep because Jesus might come and take her to heaven."

"I see." He dropped into the seat, his heart dropping, too. He thought of his beautiful and healthy daughter at school today and sent up a grateful prayer for her and for Kelsey. "I'll see what I can do about that. Can she make it in, or do you want me to drop by on my way home tonight?"

"Thanks, Dr. Kramer, but it's good for her to get out and about. We'll go for ice cream after." Kate's voice cracked, a chink in her carefully built armor. He had the feeling it was all she could to do hold on.

"Then I'll see you in twenty minutes."

"I'm getting her into the car right now." Kate said goodbye and hung up, leaving him alone with a dilemma.

He solved it by sending a text to his nurse. Run over to the drugstore and buy a stuffed animal for Kelsey, something soft for her to sleep with. This is a priority.

When he got her okay, he started the engine, motored out of the parking garage and drove the short mile to the clinic. Sunshine led the way in a sparkling glitter. The streets lay in a mantle of white like a winter wonderland, a perfect world. The hardest part of his job was that dichotomy— dealing with the tough side of life. He'd never been able to reconcile it with the beauty of life. Sometimes it was better not to try.

Ice crunched beneath his boots in the plowed back lot. He spotted Chelsea's beige sedan, obviously rescued since Monday's storm. He refused to let a single thought of her into his head. *Concentrate on work, keep your distance. Things were better that way,* he told himself.

"I hope this will work?" His nurse, Zoe, met him holding a floppy-eared stuffed bunny with big embroidered eyes and a fleecy purple coat. When he nodded, she appeared relieved. "Whew, I had to run the whole way but I beat the Koffmans here. They just pulled into the parking lot."

"Would you mind heading outside to help Kelsey in through the back?"

"No problem." Zoe bobbed off, eager to help.

Grateful to her, he tucked the rabbit in one arm and headed to his office.

Warm, still air met him in the darkened room. He stripped off his coat, tweaked the blinds open to let in a view of the back lot. A flash of red caught his eye. No need to wonder who it was from. He knew before he drew back the envelope's flap and spotted the sparkly stickers. If he breathed deep, the faint combination of strawberries and vanilla tickled his nose and sparked a familiarity he'd rather deny.

Chelsea. A variety of emotions he didn't want to explain gathered like a force in his chest, whirling like a blizzard in full blow.

His cell chimed with a text. He hauled his phone from his pocket to check the screen.

The wife is forcing me to give up my extra activities, Dr. Steve Swift had written. Can you imagine?

It's about time, Michael typed back. You need to rest so your leg can heal.

So I keep hearing. This means I need someone to take my spot on the church's Christmas food drive. I'm electing you. Aren't you honored?

Michael broke into a smile. Very. I don't have enough to do.

Just add it to your list. I'll tell the reverend you're in. Thanks, Michael. I owe ya.

That's what I'm counting on when vacation time rolls around. He hit Send, pocketed his phone and meant to grab the stuffed bunny from his desk but grabbed the stickers instead.

What was wrong with him, taking a second look? Kittens in all colors and poses grinned up at him, wreathed in bows, chasing glittering ribbon, peering out of the top of Christmas stockings. Macie would love them.

A glimmer of feeling for the gorgeous new doctor broke out of the storm of emotion in his chest, but he deftly ignored it, grabbed the stuffed rabbit and strode to the door. A quick turn of the knob and he bolted into the hall and nearly ran down a tall, slender figure. He breathed in strawberries and vanilla and froze.

"Dr. Kramer." Chelsea stared up at him. "Guess we need a stoplight in the hall."

"Or a traffic guard." What kind of response was that? He'd never been suave with the ladies, but that was pathetic. Worse, his cerebral cortex froze and he stared at her, gaping like a fish out of water. "Uh…the stickers must be from you."

"Yes, glad you found them. Johanna brought them over." The woman waltzed away, a chart tucked in the curve of her arm. Her light chestnut locks shimmered like satin beneath the florescent lights. "I like your bunny. Do you always carry him around the office?"

"It's for a patient," he clipped out before he realized she was gently kidding him.

At the far end of the hall she stopped to toss over her shoulder, "Yeah, I kind of figured that. I've got patients waiting."

"Me, too," he muttered to no one because she'd already whipped away in a swirl of white coat, gray slacks and her lustrous hair.

His feet carried him forward without the rest of him being aware of it. He found himself at the end of the short hall, giving way to the long row of exam rooms. For a moment, the emotions he fought surfaced, bringing with them the warmth of connection he'd felt with Chelsea that day he'd driven her to the diner. Dangerous feelings.

He tamped them down. All it took was a little willpower and that evening was forgotten. His heart was a quiet and safe zone once again. He halted at the hand sanitizer dispenser before shouldering into the exam room.

"Dr. Mike!" Seven-year-old Kelsey wore a purple knit hat to hide her bald head, but her smile shone bright. "What's that you got there?"

"You mean Nancy?" He tucked the bunny into her reaching arms. "She's a very good friend of mine, and she's looking for a new home."

"She is?" Kelsey wiggled with excitement in her wheelchair, clutching the blanket covering her closer.

"When she told me she wanted to live with a great little girl, I thought of you." He winked at Mrs. Koffman. "Your mom told me you were having trouble sleeping."

"I guess." Kelsey stroked the top of the bunny's head, as if she were a pet. "I don't want to get sicker and leave my mom and dad."

"I understand that. I don't want you to, either." Remission could be an elusive thing, and her kidneys were compromised. He knelt to tuck an edge of the blanket around Kelsey's knees to help keep her warmer. "Nancy is a special bunny. Didn't I tell you? She'll stay guard over you while you sleep and keep you safe in your bed."

"Really?"

"Really." He suspected angels were the ones keeping her safe, but the bunny could help, right? He patted Kelsey's knee before opening her chart.

"Thank you," Kate Koffman whispered, wiping tears from her eyes.

"All in a day's work." He tucked away the last emotion from his heart so he could face the results of his little patient's blood work.

Chapter Seven

The cell on the desk beside her chimed, echoing in the relative quiet of the after-hours clinic and startling Chelsea from her work. She saved the computer file, took off her headset and glanced at her phone.

U R still at work? Sara Beth wrote.

Yep. She turned off her computer and pushed away from the desk. The rolling wheels of her chair squeaked. I'm leaving now.

Great. I'll keep UR supper warm.

Oops. Was it that late already? Sure enough, when she checked the time it was after six o'clock. Crazy, because she hadn't even noticed time passing. Proof that she loved her job. It felt good to do what you were meant to. She grabbed her bag and keys, stuffed her iPad into her bag and burst into the hallway. The security lights made things shadowy and the big building seemed to echo around her. Was she the only one left? No, because a yellow bar of light shone under an office door. And not just any office door.

Michael was still here? And this was the bigger question, did she want to be alone with him? Uh, no. She had no idea why he stirred her up like a ladle in a soup kettle swirling everything around and around, a whirlpool of emotions. And after seeing him with that purple bunny meant for his frail little patient, well, maybe it would be best to skedaddle before he decided to come out of his office and catch her staring in his direction.

Men were trouble. That was her excuse and she was sticking to it. She slipped into the break room and freed her coat from its hanger. Not only were men trouble, they didn't stop there. They messed up your life, they got in the way of your plans and they cost you your dreams. She knew from personal experience—not that she wanted to think about *that*.

After a fast swoop to recover the remains of her lunch from the fridge, she bolted toward the door. Whoops! She caught sight of a tall, dark figure in the dim hallway and screeched to a halt before she crashed into him. Good thing, or she would have landed against the muscled plane of his chest. And why did that thought make her face burn?

"Guess I should have made more noise," he quipped. Was he blushing a little, too, or was that a trick of the shadowy light? "I thought I was the only one here. Usually I am."

"I had a lot of paperwork." She couldn't exactly make eye contact, and maybe it was better not to. Keep it professional, keep it simple, leave her emotions out of it. "It was a busy clinic day. I saw little Kelsey leaving with her bunny. I lent a hand at the back door."

"That was nice of you. Just so you know, the bunny was for medicinal purposes."

"I didn't doubt it for a minute." Hard to ignore the warm pang in her chest remembering the girl hugging the stuffed rabbit as her mom rolled her down the walkway. Chelsea had hurried to help load the girl and the chair into the van. "Is it hard dealing with critically ill children all the time?"

"It isn't easy." He didn't make eye contact either as he set the alarm. "You get used to it. Doctor objectivity and all that."

"I see." She didn't want to argue, but his purple bunny had seemed the polar opposite of cold and impartial. Michael Kramer had a gentle heart, although he clearly did his best to hide it.

He held open the outside door for her as the alarm beeped, marking time. She swept past him into the cold night air, waiting as Michael locked the door behind them with a twist of his wrist and a jangle of his key chain. Maybe it was better if she didn't break the silence. Keep it easy, keep it light, don't let him know what she really thought.

"Have a nice weekend." He nodded in her direction. A muscle tensed along his jawline and for a moment it looked as if he were going to say something more and changed his mind. He headed toward his shiny SUV, several empty parking rows away from her iced-over Toyota.

Wintry winds burned her face as she crunched toward her car. This polite professionalism was exactly the relationship she wanted with Dr. Michael Kramer. Yes, this was just the way it should be. She dug her keys out of her pocket, chipped ice out of the keyhole and started the engine, which coughed reluctantly to life. That couldn't be a good sign, but it started, so she was calling it good.

An electronic chime sang across the lot. Michael's cell. She trudged around to her trunk, wrenched it open and dug out her ice scraper, doing her best not to watch the man through her lashes. Correct that—she didn't *mean* to watch, but her eyes naturally roved his way. Call her curious and, maybe, just a little bit nosy.

"Is everything okay?" She chiseled a peephole on the windshield. Shards of ice flew everywhere.

"It's fine." He looked relieved about that. "Just a text from my mother."

"Is she watching Macie for you?" Not that it was her business, but again, curious.

"Yes, and bless her for that." He tucked his phone in his pocket and clicked open the back door. "No, it's about Macie's Christmas present."

That sounded familiar, so she searched her memory banks. "Oh, right. The kitten."

"I've said no for years, and kittens were everywhere we went." He dug out his scraper and began shaving ice off the windows. "Mom's friends had cats with kittens. They were advertised in the paper, given away in front of the grocery store but now when I've finally given in, not one anywhere."

"Have you tried the animal shelter?"

"Mom's last resort, after calling her friends and people they knew. Everyone is out of little kittens which Macie has her heart set on." He jabbed a big shard of ice free from his windshield. "Hey, your dad's a veterinarian."

"And two of my sisters. I could ask them if they know of any available baby felines." She dropped her scraper on the car's hood and dug into her pocket. "I'll do it right now before I forget."

"Thanks, Chelsea." Relief softened the hard angles of his face. He really was a handsome man.

"No problem." She tapped a quick message to Johanna. Michael had turned his back to her, working his way around his vehicle. *Don't notice the striking line of his shoulders,* she told herself. *You're in denial, remember? Maybe it would be better if you got in the car, stopped looking at him, and let the defrosters do all the work instead.*

Her chiming phone stopped her. A quick look told her that it was from Johanna. Apparently a quick escape was not meant to be. She squinted at the screen, scanning the text. "Guess what? I've got good news."

"That was fast." His hint of a smile dazzled even from across the parking lot. Good thing her defenses were up. Way up. Fortress strong.

"My sisters are apparently hooked into the kitten market." She held up her phone. "A cat named Mrs. Pickles had kittens four weeks ago and the owner is looking for good homes for them. I've got an address and a number."

"That's the best news I've had all day." His hint of a smile grew, promising dimples.

Since his dimples might knock down her defenses in one swift blow, she scrolled through her text messages for the one Steve had sent her a while back, with everyone's numbers. She spotted Michael's and tapped in the number. "I'll just send you the info. Johanna says you have to go over right now if you're serious."

"As in this exact minute?"

"She says there are only two unclaimed kittens and they're going fast. The cat owner's had a

lot of interest. Christmas kittens are in demand."
Chelsea hit Send. There. Her obligation was done.
Michael could get a kitten and she could zip home,
have dinner and hang with her sisters. Whatever
energy she had left over, she'd use to keep him
out of her thoughts.

"Okay, then I guess I'd better look at kittens."
He frowned at his phone, tapping in a message.
"I'm sure my mother won't mind keeping Macie
a little longer. I'm going to need some advice on
cats."

"Hey, don't look at me. I'm not a vet." But she
was hungry, her growling stomach reminded her.
Just another reason to escape while she could. She
yanked open her door and leaned in, flicking the
defroster on high. "I'm not a cat expert."

"Right. I'm sure I can figure it out." He tucked
his phone into his coat pocket. "How hard can it
be? I'll just pick one."

"Sounds like a plan."

"And pray it's the right one."

"It will be."

"I can do that, no problem." He blew out a sigh.
The wind gusted, tousling his short brown hair
and for a moment he looked vulnerable. The cool
doctor facade slid away and he was just a dad
wanting to make his daughter happy. "Thanks for
the help, Dr. McKaslin."

"You're welcome, Dr. Kramer." See how they

were just two colleagues being friendly? Nothing to worry about. "Say hi to Macie for me."

"Will do. Good night." He straightened his spine, opened his door and angled in behind the wheel. She did the same, settling into the worn seat of her Toyota, ignoring the strange tug—on her conscience, she told herself firmly, and not on her heart.

As the defroster blasted a hole in the fog and ice on her windshield, she buckled in and flicked on her lights. A wise woman would have stopped the memory from rising to the surface, overtaking the moment and hurling her back in time, but did she stop it? No, she let her mother's remembered voice guide her into the past. She was eight years old following her sisters into the laundry room of her aunt's house.

"What sweet little things." Mom knelt down in her graceful and elegant way, her dark blond hair silky against her shoulders, and rubbed the mother cat's fluffy head. "You did a good job, Sunshine. You have beautiful babies."

The mama cat answered with a proud, rusty purr. Her green eyes closed in contentment as she lay curled up on a soft blanket in her basket with newborn kittens sleeping against her.

"Girls, come close and see but don't touch yet. Just one at a time," Mom instructed in her kind way. "Chelsea, you first."

Mom's touch was warm and comforting, guiding Chelsea down beside her onto the warm tile floor. Currents from the furnace ruffled the edge of the blanket and puffed warm air across her face as she knelt, forefinger out, simply aching to touch those wee, fragile little beings. She'd never felt anything as soft as she stroked a white paw. Her whole heart melted like butter on a stack of hot pancakes.

"What do you think, baby?" Mom asked. "Which one do you like?"

"I dunno. I like 'em all." She touched a little black paw and then an orange striped one. The newborns didn't stir, sound asleep, tucked safely against their mama's tummy. She loved every one of them so much.

"Too bad you can't have 'em all." Dad chuckled, with toddler Johanna on his hip, all dark curls and big, curious brown eyes. "Can you imagine? A house full of girls and kittens?"

"No, don't even put the idea in their heads, Grant. Honestly." Mom's lilting chuckle made everyone smile, even four-year-old Meg clinging to Dad's pant leg. "We'll start with two. Two Christmas kittens. You get to pick one, Chelsea. Sara Beth, your turn. Gently now, with just your finger."

"Yes, Mommy." Sweet Sara Beth knelt beside Chelsea, her cute face serious as she traced a kitten's tiny foot. "I pick the snowy one. She's just like Christmas."

"I like the orange one," Chelsea decided, gazing at the itty-bitty feline face scrunched up in sleep. "She's like my Christmas stocking. Striped."

Mom and Dad's laughter evaporated as the memory faded. Chelsea blinked, finding herself seated in her car, the past long gone, and the defroster blowing. Her chest ached with a mix of love and loss for what once was. Mom felt so far away, wherever heaven was, and she swiped at her eyes, surprised to find them damp.

Michael's snazzy SUV rolled by in the dark evening, the dash lights illuminating his perfect profile. Don't do it, she told herself. You don't have to help him. It isn't your business. He was smart enough to make it through medical school, he's smart enough to pick out a kitten.

But what did she do when she put her car in gear? Did she head left out of the lot to go home? No, she went right, following the flash of Michael's taillights on the shadowed side street. Helping him was the right thing to do. He did so much for sick and defenseless children. He shouldn't have to pick out his daughter's Christmas gift alone.

Michael spotted the sedan in his rearview. What was Chelsea—Dr. McKaslin—doing? His forehead drew tight with the force of his frown. He called her, keeping his attention on the icy road. His vehicle did a slow-motion halt at the intersection. He listened on speaker to her phone ring and watched her in the rearview mirror, able to see the soft shine of her hair and the heart-shape of her face through the glass.

"Hello, Michael." Her alto held a businesslike tone.

Businesslike, he could do. "Hey, you're following me."

"It's a total coincidence."

"Is that so?" He checked the light—still red—and focused on his mirror again. "You just happen to be going my way?"

"Something like that. I haven't seen Mrs. Collins in some time. Thought I should drop by."

"Mrs. Collins? Oh, right. The lady with the kittens." He glanced up to see the green light shining at him. Not sure how long it had been that color, he checked the intersection before creeping ahead. It wasn't proof Chelsea—Dr. McKaslin—distracted him. He was just…what was the word? Grateful. That was it. Grateful she wanted to help out. "It's nice of you to take time out of your evening."

"I told you. I wanted to check in on Mrs. Collins anyway. She's a longtime client of my family's vet clinic. It seemed like a good idea."

"Okay." He heard what she didn't say. Maybe what she couldn't. Behind the cold wall around his heart, he felt a pinch of gratitude. It was nice she wanted to help him, but why did it have to be her?

"Turn left at the next intersection," she advised.

"Got it." His jaw clamped tight as he slowed and signaled. When he flicked his eyes up to the mirror, there she was, signaling in the lane behind him.

She really was very beautiful. Why couldn't he stop noticing?

Eyes ahead, pay attention to the road, don't look back, he told himself, crossing the lane of traffic and rambling down the snowy residential street. He spotted the house on the corner a block in, swathed in multicolored lights. He parked at the curb.

"I got some more info from Johanna." Once she'd parked, Chelsea picked her way toward him, her keys in hand, elegant as poetry in the faint shine of the overhead streetlight. Surrounded by white, wrapped up in navy wool and a red scarf, she made a breathtaking picture. "The kittens will be ready to leave their mama in two weeks, on Christmas Eve day. Is that perfect timing or what?"

"Perfect," he muttered, thinking of her.

"Why, hello there, little Chelsea McKaslin all grown up." A woman opened the front door, her oval face friendly, her hair a bob of silver. "I haven't seen you since your college days."

"I haven't been around much since then. It's good to see you." Chelsea led the way up the steps and into the light. "I've been a tad busy in the meantime."

"Becoming a doctor, yes, I've heard all about it. Your dad does nothing but boast about his girls every time I'm in the clinic." Kindly, Mrs. Collins stepped back, holding the door for them. "Brr, it's cold out there. Come in where it's warm. You must be Dr. Kramer."

"It's good to meet you, ma'am." He stripped off his gloves in the heat of the house. The Craftsman-style home boasted impressive woodwork and a Christmas tree lit up in front of a bay window. More colorful lights flashed and glowed. "I guess you know why I'm here."

"Your little girl wants a kitten for Christmas." Mrs. Collins' brown eyes glimmered with approval. "And what fine kittens they are, just like their mama. I've got two kittens left, just adorable as can be. Follow me into the laundry room. I have to keep them contained so they don't get into trouble and hurt themselves, the dear things."

A few steps through the kitchen, where the scent of bread baking filled the air, and the older lady opened a door. Inside was a very large laundry room and a comfy basket with a calico cat curled up in it, presumably Mrs. Pickles. Six-week-old kittens in various colors sped across the tile floor after a rolling toy ball with a bell in it. All five of them looked up at the newcomers, abandoned their game and romped over with friendly curiosity. They were so little. What kind of care would a kitten need?

"Oh, what sweeties." Beside him, Chelsea settled on the floor. Kittens tumbled into her lap, reached their paws up her sweater and tried to climb onto her shoulders. "Hello, there. How could anyone choose just one of you?"

Their tiny answering mews drowned out her low, musical laughter. She scooped up a calico and cradled it against her cheek, her gentleness so beautiful he couldn't find the words to describe it.

"Everyone has a home except for the little calico you're holding, Chelsea, and this little guy." Mrs. Collins pointed out a black kitten with a patch of white on his belly. "He's a love. The tip of his ear is missing. He was born that way, but with extra heart."

"Poor little guy." Chelsea scooped the black one up with her other hand. He snuggled her cheek, eyes full of love. "You're so *cute*."

What should he do? Michael frowned. Macie distinctly wanted a white kitty, or, more recently, a gray striped one like the McKaslin's cat, Burt.

These two were neither.

"How can anyone frown when they're standing

in a room of kittens?" Chelsea shook her head, scattering her thick silken hair.

"Call me gifted," he quipped. "I don't know which one to pick. She wanted a striped one."

"It's a dilemma." She set the little ones down and gave a nearby cat toy a toss. The little blue ball rolled, the bell inside jingled and all five baby felines bounced after it, tails up, ears perked, eyes bright. Five sets of wee paws pounced. "The black kitten is a love, the calico is sweet."

"Which one would Macie pick?" He had no idea. Something tugged on his trouser leg. A little black face peered up at him, green eyes bright with a silent plea. The kitten may have been asking, pick me. Love me.

Not that he was going to let his heart melt or anything, but he scooped up the creature with care. Tiny whiskers twitched, the kitten wriggled, so alive and warm in his hand. Wee claws caught his shirt as the miniature feline curled in, snuggling beneath Michael's chin.

"I sort of like this one," he confessed. "But Macie wants a girl."

"That is a dilemma, sure." Chelsea rose and came closer, swirling in to pet the kitten. "But there is an easy solution."

"Huh?" Words temporarily eluded him as he breathed in her strawberry-vanilla scent. The strawberry was from her shampoo, he realized when a lock of her hair brushed his jaw. The vanilla must be from her lotion. He sure wished he hadn't noticed.

"Isn't it obvious?" She looked down, laughing at a kitten trying to climb her pants leg. "Get them both."

"Both? What? No, sorry. Two cats? I can't do it. I'm not sure about getting just one." Although he had to admit the little guy was nice. "I'm not an animal person. Never have been. I have no idea what caring for one takes."

"Two wouldn't be much more trouble than one." She cradled the cute calico beneath her chin. "Think of it this way. Macie will get twice the love in return. Doesn't she deserve that?"

"You are starting to annoy me, Dr. McKaslin." He shook his head, feigning disapproval. "You make it impossible to say no. I have to take them both now."

"Awesome. And this way they'll have each other and won't be lonely when Macie's at school." Chelsea kissed the top of the calico's fluffy head, so soft, and gently set the baby on the ground. Sweet eyes blinked up at her before the kitten leaped off to join her siblings in play. So cute. Macie was going to get two great new friends. "I'll get a list of the things you'll need from Dad's clinic. They have new-kitten information and care info. It should answer all your questions. If not, just ask."

"That's a big relief. You have no idea." He lowered the kitten he held to the ground, letting him go. The sweet little black scampered away bounding with kitten joy. "Thanks, Chelsea."

"Hey, I didn't do this for you. I did it for the kittens. That's all." A likely excuse she hoped he would believe. "They need a good home."

"And Macie needs them." He flashed a real smile, not just the hint of one, and it curved the corners of his mouth to perfection. The promise of his dimples was nothing compared to the reality of them.

Wow. Double wow.

Was she in trouble now.

Chapter Eight

Chelsea checked her cell as she sat at the desk in her room, where she used to do her homework as a girl and stared at the screen. No messages. That was a good sign for a Saturday midmorning when she was on call. She focused on her tablet computer and the day's to-do list that was getting longer by the minute. It wasn't the length that was stymieing her. It was the next item up. *Get kitten info to Michael.*

Like even thinking of him was a good idea. She shook her head, staring out the window at the horse barn and fenced pasture. The frosted white roll of the Wyoming plains spread out in a glittering, icy wonder. A powder-blue sky stretched from horizon to horizon and she wanted to be out in it, maybe rolling a snowball to toss at one of her sisters or riding her horse. But that wouldn't get her to-do list whittled down. Work first, then play.

"Hey," Meg clamored through the doorway. "You busy?"

"What does it look like?" She gestured to her computer.

"Hey, don't try the I'm-working excuse with me. I saw you staring out the window." She plopped onto the foot of the bed, her long dark hair pulled back in a single ponytail.

"I wasn't staring. I was thinking." About trying *not* to think about Michael. Chelsea scooted around in her chair, resting her chin on the top of the backrest. "What are you up to?"

"Nothing good. I'm bored."

"I can give you half my list to do."

"Funny." Meg leaned back, stretching out on the bedspread. "Johanna, is that you?"

"It's me." Footsteps preceded the youngest McKaslin sister, who tromped into the room and tumbled onto the bed crossways, her sleek dark hair bouncing. "Whew, this feels good. Doing nothing. I could get used to it."

"Me, too," Meg agreed, tucking her hands behind her head.

"Guess who I just talked to?" Johanna's words held a note of delight. And, more likely, doom. The twist of foreboding in Chelsea's middle warned her as Johanna continued happily on. "Mrs. Collins."

"Oh, I love her," Meg enthused. "Her Mrs. Pickles is the sweetest cat."

"I know. I dropped by to check on her and the kittens at home after they were born." Johanna levered herself up on one elbow. "Adorable. Mrs. Pickles is one of my favorite patients."

"Did Mrs. Collins say anything about, let's say, a handsome doctor stopping by to pick out a kitten?" Meg asked, way too innocently.

"Why, yes, she did." Johanna's dark eyes twinkled merrily. "And guess what? She also happened to mention that the handsome doctor didn't arrive alone."

"Is that right?" Meg looked as if she were thoroughly enjoying herself. Downstairs the house phone rang, but nobody moved to get it. "Could he have been accompanied by someone we know?"

"As a matter of fact, he was," Johanna replied. "But did our dear sister tell us about it? No. Not one single word."

"That's a shame really."

"You know, it really is."

"Okay, Chelsea. Inquiring minds want to know." Meg rolled over and propped herself up on both elbows. "So, spill. We're not leaving it alone until you do."

"That's right," Johanna concurred. "You might as well tell us now."

"I cannot believe you two." Chelsea rolled her eyes heavenward, hoping for patience. "Honestly, you two are leaping to conclusions. Michael, I mean Dr. Kramer, didn't know anything about choosing a kitten. I helped him out, that's all. It was a favor. Colleague to colleague."

"That's not what Mrs. Collins said." Johanna waggled her brows. "Apparently Michael couldn't stop looking at you."

"At me? I didn't notice that. No way." Honestly. And just because she was blushing didn't mean she wanted it to be true because, of course, it wasn't. "Okay, fine, I admit he was looking at me, but I was holding a kitten at the time—"

"She protests too much," Meg interrupted.

"Way too much," Johanna agreed.

"That was Dad on the phone." Sara Beth poked her head in, her rich brown hair clipped back by two barrettes. "He said things are glacial at the clinic."

"Good, he could use the time off," Meg piped in.

"So he's closing up after his current patient and heading over to the tree farm." Sara Beth crossed the room and plopped into the overstuffed chair by the desk. "He wants us meet him to pick out a Christmas tree. Can you believe it?"

"Oh, poor Dad. He's trying hard this year." Meg's face fell. "I know it's tough for him."

"We're all trying hard this year," Johanna agreed. But Christmas would never be the same. Chelsea held back the words she knew her sisters were all thinking. If only she'd taken leave for their last Christmas all together. If she could go back in time, she'd have done it differently. Put her schooling on hold, spent more time with Mom, who despite her fight had passed away suddenly and unexpectedly. Everyone had thought there was more time.

"I have an idea." Johanna popped up on the bed, crossing her legs. "Why don't we ride to town? The horses have been shut up in the stable with the storms and they could use the exercise. We can take the back way along the river to the tree farm."

"Awesome idea," Meg seconded, bounding to her feet.

"Let's saddle up." Sara Beth pushed out of the chair. "I'll text Dad. You're coming, Chelsea. Right?"

"And give up the chance to go riding? You're kidding, right?" She turned off her tablet, but the next item on her to-do list caught her eye before the screen went black. Michael Kramer.

What was she going to do about liking the man? Well, it looked like she wouldn't have to solve the problem at this very second. Sometimes it was good to put off what you didn't want to do. She was more than happy to clomp out of the room after her sisters and down the stairs.

* * *

One good thing about the weekend was spending time with his daughter. Michael folded a load of towels in the laundry room, glad there was another benefit to the weekend. No chance of seeing Chelsea McKaslin until Monday. With the door open, he had a perfect view of the kitchen and family room where Macie sorted through the two boxes of ornaments he'd carried down from the attic.

"I like the sparkly ones." She held up a box of glitter covered candy cane ornaments. Her cast now sported the new stickers Chelsea had left on his desk.

Chelsea. There she was again, front and center in his thoughts. There didn't seem to be any way to escape her. Not at all sure what to do about that, he folded the last towel, dropped it into the laundry basket and closed the dryer door.

He shouldered out the laundry room and dropped the basket on the corner of the kitchen island. "Are you ready to go, Mace?"

"Yep!" She set down the ornament with care, surveying the open boxes full of Christmas things. "I got everything ready, Daddy. We can put the tree right here. You're gonna decorate it, too, right?"

"Right." His decorating skills left much to be desired, but he'd muddled through last year. He could do it again this year. "Grab your coat and let's roll."

"Yay!" She'd already launched herself across the room, sneakers pounding.

Not quite as enthusiastic, he grabbed his cell from the counter, his keys from his pocket and followed his daughter. She sat on a bench by the door into the garage, trying to tug on her pink winter boots. Not easy with a cast, so he knelt to help.

His phone rang. Bad timing, since it was a call from the service. "What is it, Janice?"

"Mrs. Lansing," the operator answered with cool efficiency. "It's about Howie."

"Howie." He blew out a sigh, thinking of the little boy and his fight with bone cancer, still in the hospital. So many things could go wrong after a surgery like his. Shields up, Michael braced himself for every bad possibility. "Do I need to come in?"

"No, Mrs. Lansing said Howie wanted to tell you his arm feels better now that the cancer was cut out."

"Thanks for letting me know." His throat closed up. He couldn't say anything more, so he disconnected. Emotions threatened, but he couldn't let one of them in.

"Do I have to go to Grammy's now?" Macie lifted her chin, bravely struggling with disappointment.

"No, I don't have to go. We can still get your tree together."

"It's *our* tree, Daddy." She hopped off the bench, dragging her coat with her into the garage.

His daughter's gentle correction burrowed through him, leaving him feeling inadequate, the way he had since Diana passed. He set the home security alarm and closed the door while Macie climbed into the backseat. He hurried to help her get settled, the glittery stickers on her cast glinting in the ambient light. He loved spending time with her. Maybe the new memories they could make together would be as good as the older ones, in their own way.

The drive to the tree farm at the edge of town was uneventful. He found a radio station playing Christmas music, according to Macie's instructions. It looked like he wasn't the only one with the idea to buy a tree. The place was jammed. Not surprising, since there was only one more Saturday before Christmas.

"Daddy, look!" Macie unclicked her seat belt and clamored out into the cold. She gestured across the lot where four horses and riders ambled to a stop at the edge of the lot.

Wait a minute. His gaze shot straight to the rider in the second position, her light chestnut locks gleaming in the golden sunlight. No, it couldn't be. His pulse skidded to a stop. His palms broke out in a sweat.

"Macie!" Chelsea's alto carried to him on the breeze as she dismounted. "Hey, it's great to see you."

"Are you getting a tree, too?" Sara Beth asked as her boots hit the ground.

"Yep. Me and my dad." Macie shot out of the backseat and slammed the door.

Chelsea. What was she doing here? He was not ready for this, not after yesterday. He rubbed his aching forehead, took his time extracting his key and locking up. Four women's voices joined the girl's sweet high voice, but only one alto stood out above all the others.

That couldn't be a good sign. He crunched through the snow around the back of the SUV and closed Macie's door. With his heart thudding in his chest like a bass guitar, he knew he couldn't put it off any longer. The instant he looked up, his gaze centered on Chelsea, her face pink from the wind, blue eyes bright and beautiful.

"Michael." Her friendly greeting invited him closer, invited him in, as if she didn't feel the snap of connection that tried to open his heart to her.

Great. Well, at least this was one-sided and much easier to deal with that way. So all he had to do was implement his defensive strategy, that of mind over matter, willpower over emotions, and he'd be fine. Just fine, and forget about the fact it hadn't worked so well in Mrs. Collins's laundry room.

"Funny meeting you here." Chelsea blinked up at him. "I guess great minds think alike."

"That and it's the only tree farm in town."

"True." She laid a gloved hand on her horse's nose in an unconscious caring gesture. The tobiano paint, sporting beautiful white and bay patterns, gazed at her with adoration, of course. Who wouldn't? "Wow, Macie. Your cast is especially snazzy."

"I know. Thank you so much for them." The girl proudly showed off her sticker work. "I love all the kittens."

"Me, too," Chelsea agreed.

Sara Beth sidled in. "Chels, I'm gonna interrupt and take Rio for you."

"Thanks bunches." Chelsea handed over the reins.

"We'll get her blanketed," Meg promised brightly. "Right, Johanna?"

"Absolutely. C'mon, girl." Johanna clucked to the mare and Rio followed obediently. "Macie, do you want to help?"

"Yes!"

"Then come with us." As they walked away, Meg waggled her brows and Johanna sent Chelsea a wink on their way toward a pole safely off the lot, a good place to tie and blanket the animals.

Her sisters. Chelsea rolled her eyes. She wasn't exactly sure what was wrong with them. It may be undiagnosable, or mental. Surely they understood she was not ready for a relationship. Not even close.

"I meant to email you the kitten information." She said the first thing that popped into her head. The trouble was, her brain didn't seem to be working well. "I didn't get a chance to this morning. I was on housecleaning rotation."

And then I wanted to put off emailing you.

"Christmas is thirteen days away. We have time." He shoved his hands into his coat pockets. "It was nice of you to come with me last night."

"It was nothing. Just a favor among colleagues." Or, at least, that was all she would admit. "You must be anxious for Macie to meet her new kittens."

"I think they'll make her happy."

"And vice versa." The sun brightened, radiating around her with a surreal glow. All around them, cars drove into the lot and children dashed ahead of their parents shouting and laughing, but it was all background to Michael. He stayed front and center. All she could see, all she could hear was him.

"I had to coordinate with my folks," he explained. "Mom is going to keep Macie a few hours on Christmas Eve day while I run over to pick up the kittens. We'll hide them in Mom's laundry room for the night and my folks will bring them over early Christmas morning."

"Sounds like you'll be able to keep it a surprise."

"That's the plan, anyway. Their mewing has the potential to give us away." Love for his daughter softened his granite features, showing a hint of a tender man with a caring heart.

"Chelsea? Michael?" A woman's pleasant voice came out of nowhere. The world came back into focus as Dr. Susan Benedict ambled over with a credit card in hand. "Fancy running into you here. You two are Christmas tree shopping, too?"

"Just arrived." Chelsea wasn't sure, but was she blushing? Her face felt hot. "It looks like everyone's here today. It's a madhouse."

"It is. Fred is loading my tree for me now. I was lucky to get here early before things got busy." Susan brushed a lock of blond hair out of her eyes. "So, you two are here together?"

"What? Uh, the two of us? No." Chelsea's tongue tied. Did her face feel even redder? "We're both here, but we're—"

"Not here *together,*" Michael finished, looking just as uncomfortable as she felt. "I'm here with my daughter."

"I'm here with my sisters. And my dad. There he is." The idea of her and Michael *together?* Crazy. She *so* could not imagine it. And yes, her face definitely was blazing red. She could see the tip of her nose as red as a Rudolph's. Good thing Dad was walking over, the perfect distraction. She waved at the burly, dark-haired man heading her way.

"Hi, Michael, hi, Susan. There's my girl." Dark hair thinning on top, round face, ready smile, that was her dad. "Good to see you out and about, Chels. You're my workaholic."

"I might be a chip off the old block, but I'm not a workaholic." She rolled her eyes. Why did everyone keep saying that? "I just like to work."

"Hey, I get it," Michael said amicably. "Me, too. Grant, how are things at the vet clinic?"

"A little slow. Had a dog who helped himself to the Christmas baking. Chocolate, you know, but he'll be fine. They rushed him in right away. Hi there, Susan."

"Hello, Grant. Well, it looks like they have my tree loaded. I'd better get going. Good to see all of you, together or not." Susan gave Chelsea a wink before crunching through the icy snow toward her SUV.

A wink? Why a wink? "We're not together," she told her dad before he could ask.

"Absolutely not," Michael confirmed, his gaze finding hers with a conspiratorial look.

"I don't know why people are asking that." She found herself smiling at him. Smiling. And the feeling she'd been fighting since Mrs. Collins's laundry room zoomed back with the force of a tornado. Boom, it struck her hard in the middle, rattling her ribs and her heart, leaving her rocking on her feet. Good thing she excelled at denial. "I mean, you and me?"

"I'm clearly not your type." Humor looked good on him.

Not that she was noticing. "Definitely. Plus, I'm not looking. At all. Forget it."

"Okay, okay." Grant held up both hands in surrender. "I won't ask what you two are doing here together. What do I know?"

"Daddy!" Macie bounded up her to father. "Are we gonna get the tree now?"

"I guess that's why we're here. May as well get a tree." Michael changed when he ruffled his daughter's flyaway hair. The granite softened, his reserve eased and he looked like a whole new man. He'd been handsome before, but add a dash of tenderness and wow.

Total and complete wow.

"Hi, Mr. McKaslin." Macie grinned up at Grant. "See my cast?"

"I haven't seen a decorating job that good. Ever."

Grant took a moment to admire the plethora of shiny stickers stuck to pink plaster. "Very Christmassy."

"Plus, I want a kitten for Christmas this year, you know."

"So I've heard."

"This way I can look at kittens even though I don't have one." Macie peered up through her lashes at her dad, as if trying to read his reaction. "But I'm getting one, right?"

"Sorry, that's one mystery best left for Christmas morning." Michael wrapped a powerful arm around his daughter's slight shoulders, gently tugged her away. "C'mon, Mace, let's leave the McKaslins to tree hunt. You get to pick ours this year."

"All by myself?"

"Yes, all by yourself. Hope I don't regret it." Although he spoke to her whole family, who gathered around her like a half moon, his gaze found only her. For a split second the unguardedness in his eyes remained, revealing a hint of the real Michael Kramer. Her heart lurched, still stuck in suspended animation, while he tucked his daughter's hand in his and walked away.

"Earth to Chelsea." Meg nudged her. It would have to be Meg who noticed she couldn't drag her attention away from the handsome man disappearing into a row of evergreens.

"Sorry. It's all this free time. I don't know what to do with myself." Her joke made everyone laugh.

"C'mon, let's start looking." Grant sounded like Christmas cheer itself, but his smile looked too wide and too forced. Poor Dad, he really was trying hard to make this like any Christmas.

But this wasn't. It would never be again.

"How about that one?" Johanna pointed to a scrubby Charlie Brown tree, growing lopsided and stunted. "The poor thing. It's so cute."

"Johanna, you always go for the underdog." Grant's chuckle rumbled warmly and full of a father's love.

"I know, I can't help myself." She shrugged, her soft brown hair framing her lovely face perfectly.

"I'm in the mood for something grand. Let's go all-out." He looped his arm around Johanna's shoulder and they headed down the same row where Michael and Macie had disappeared. "Let's find the best and biggest tree on the farm. What do you say, girls?"

"Now you're talkin'." Meg sailed after them.

"This is going to be fun." Sara Beth launched down the aisle, too, leaving Chelsea behind.

The sun lit up the world, glinting off the white ground, shimmering in evergreen branches and casting dappled light over the families winding through the acres of fir and spruce. Everything felt so normal. How could that be possible? She wasn't entirely certain her heart had started beating again.

A movement grabbed her attention—a man with a black coat, a wide-shouldered stance and a little girl at his side.

Chelsea sighed. She could try all the denial she wanted, but it was futile. She did notice him. She was attracted to him. But really liking him? That was another matter entirely. Hands fisted, she willed her gaze from him and prayed that from this point on Michael Kramer would have no effect on her. Nothing. Caring deeply for him was one mistake she refused to make.

"Chels?" Sara Beth wandered over. "Are you okay?"

"Sure, I'm great." No way did she want to confess the truth. She didn't want to open up the past or to admit what she felt—and was trying not to feel—for Michael.

"I know this is hard without Mom." Sara Beth bit her bottom lip, saying nothing more and betraying everything.

"It is hard." Why hadn't she been focused on her sisters? If she had, then she would have noticed Sara Beth's pain. "C'mon, we'll look together. This grieving thing is easier when you don't do it alone."

"Exactly." Sara Beth nodded and blew out a

shaky breath. "It's just hard. There's a terrible hole without Mom."

"I know. We'll just have do the best we can. We'll get through this."

"We will," Sara Beth agreed.

Chelsea took her sister's hand and together they headed down rows of dappled sun and evergreen. *Lord, watch over my family,* she prayed. *Somehow let this Christmas heal them.*

Chapter Nine

"I got all the ornaments picked out." Macie chattered away in the backseat, revved up with excitement. "Know just how to do it. I've got a plan and everything."

"A plan, huh?" He glanced briefly in the rearview mirror, taking in her flushed face and eager eyes. His daughter had plans? And here he'd hoped she hadn't inherited that particularly tendency.

"Yep. I got it all figured out," she said happily. "First, we've got to put the tree up right away."

"What about lunch?"

"Uh." She bit her bottom lip, her face scrunching as she thought. "We'll have lunch and then put up the tree. Then we have to find the lights."

"They weren't in the boxes I brought down?"

"Nope." She shook her head, scattering windswept brown curls.

Where had Mom put them? She'd packed up the

tree decorations last year. Frowning, he eased the SUV around the corner of the residential street, slowing as he spotted kids up ahead, pulling each other on plastic saucer sleds. They parted, standing curbside as he crept past. His neighbors were out putting up lights, hauling in Christmas trees or staking metallic reindeer in their yards. It wasn't hard to spot his house. The brick Tudor, bought last year because it was a block from his parents' home, was dark as night. Not a single light shone or one decoration. It could have been Scrooge's house.

Good thing they were going to change that this weekend. He turned into the driveway and hit the garage remote. As the door cranked upward, his mind wandered to the one person he didn't want it to. Chelsea McKaslin, with her gentle friendliness, approachable beauty and her kindness. How did he stop feeling what he was trying not to feel?

He had to shut it down, overcome it, get past it somehow, some way. What he needed to do was to think of her as a colleague, and only as a colleague. Maybe if he tried hard enough and gave it enough time, eventually it might work. A man had to hope so.

He pulled into the garage, cut the engine and opened Macie's door.

"Grammy!" She scrambled onto the concrete floor in a flurry of energy.

What was wrong with him? He'd been so absorbed, he hadn't even noticed his mother pull up in her minivan. Trying to change the way he thought of Chelsea was apparently taking all his available brain cells.

"I made a casserole that should cover your lunch and supper." Mom carried a covered casserole in both hands, balancing a plastic container on top. Apparently she'd made rolls, too. "Looks like you two have been busy. That's quite a Christmas tree you have there."

"It's the biggest one that will fit in our living room. The other one was too tall," Macie explained, clomping along at her grammy's side.

While the two ladies talked, he unlocked the door, punched in the alarm code and took the food from his mom. The meal scorched through his gloves, telling him it was table-ready. "Do you want to join us, Mom?"

"No, I ate with your father. Since it's between snowstorms, he's putting Santa on the roof while he can."

"And all the reindeer, too?" Macie asked.

"Yes, can't forget reindeer." Mom went straight to the cupboards for plates and cups. "He has the nativity left to go, and that'll take him all afternoon. So I thought I'd come over and help you with your tree."

"Awesome!" Macie's delighted answer echoed

in the kitchen. The two trotted off together to set the table, and he trailed after them with the food. He couldn't seem to concentrate on what they were saying. Something about the Christmas tree. All his poor mind could do was picture Chelsea in the sunshine.

A glimmer of a wish, or at least the first seed of one, threatened to take root and grow. He grimaced, not pleased at all. He had to stop it. He tamped it down, closed off his feelings and refused to give it life. It was the smartest thing to do. Love hadn't worked out well for him, he wasn't suited to it. He had to leave it at that. Chelsea was a wish and nothing more, one not meant to come true.

"I get to say grace!" Macie dropped into her chair and folded her hands, her enthusiasm bringing him back to this moment of his life and the blessings in it.

"Okay, is it me, or is this light hanging thing a disaster?" Chelsea stepped back to take a look at the colorful twinklers on the top half of the Christmas tree. "It's lopsided."

"It really is." Sara Beth sidled up beside her to study the problem.

"It's not bad," Johanna chimed in. "*If* you squint at it."

"Or, we could turn the tree so the bad side is against the wall." Meg shouldered over to add her opinion while Burt, the gray-striped cat, looked up with interest from his perch on the back of the couch.

"This is what I get for not learning the skill from Mom." Chelsea tugged the ladder in place beside the tree. "She always insisted on doing it, remember?"

"She could wind the lights in one big swirl and they looked picture-perfect every time," Meg remembered, flipping her long brown hair behind her shoulder.

"Mom had a gift. She could have been a professional tree decorator," Johanna agreed, love for their mother tender in her voice.

"Even that last Christmas she had Dad place the lights to her exact specifications." Sara Beth sighed, falling silent. There were not words to describe the sweetness and sorrow of that last holiday when Mom had been so ill. "Okay, we'll try it again. Chelsea, up the ladder. Meg, why are you just standing there?"

"I'm supervising. Face it, you all need me." Meg smiled mischievously. "Since I'm in charge—"

"Who appointed you?" Johanna asked.

"If anyone's in charge it should be me," Johanna quipped. "I'm artistic."

"But I'm the oldest," Chelsea chimed in. "Although I'd be happy to abdicate supervisory status—"

"Dibs," Meg called out. "And now that that's settled, I say a cookie break for everyone."

"I like how you think." Johanna pirouetted and led the way toward the kitchen. Dee, napping by the crackling fireplace, hopped up to follow. "Those bakery cookies I got yesterday are addictive. I think it's the sprinkles."

"And the icing." Meg rushed to catch up with her. "Do you know what would go great with them?"

"Hot chocolate," Johanna's voice echoed from the kitchen.

"Chelsea, what's wrong? I know you're not upset about the lights," Sara Beth said in her gentle, understanding tone. "This is hard without Mom, isn't it?"

"Yes." It was. "I miss her. She loved Christmas."

"I know. If she were here right now, you know she'd be singing carols and conducting us in three-part harmony. She made everything just right." Sara Beth paused. "But that's not the only thing bothering you, is it?"

"No." If only she could admit the truth, but the words were stuck in her throat, refusing to be spoken.

"I saw how it was at the tree farm." Sara Beth lowered her voice. "With Michael."

"I wish it wasn't like that with Michael." There.

She'd actually said the words. That was a big step, right there. "You have no idea how much I wish it."

"I can tell." Sara Beth moved closer, caught Chelsea's hand and squeezed gently. "Why are you fighting so hard?"

"I have my reasons." She'd made one big confession. That didn't mean she was ready for another.

"You haven't dated since Nick. That was a long time ago." Sara Beth apparently had it already figured out.

"Sorry, I'm still not going to talk about it." Chelsea managed what she hoped was a smile. Life went on, broken hearts mended and she'd been busy achieving her goals. "Who has time for dudes anyway?"

"Right. We're busy here." Sara Beth tugged her in the direction of the kitchen. "Busy with hot chocolate and cookies."

"And no time to talk about dudes." She guessed Sara Beth understood more than she was saying, and Chelsea appreciated her sister's solidarity. "Is that my cell ringing?"

"Sounds like it."

"Great." Just knowing it was the answering service and she'd have to go into the clinic, she dashed through the kitchen to the back door entry where she'd left her coat. As she raced by Bayly, the dog lifted his head from his bed to watch her and Dee barked, thinking it was a game. Chelsea wrenched her cell out of her coat pocket before it went to voice mail.

"Hello?" She panted into the phone.

"Chelsea?" a man's voice boomed. "It's Steve."

"Steve?" And not the answering service. Awesome. Which meant she'd be able to hang with her sisters over cookies and cocoa after all. Yay.

"Did I call at a bad time?" he asked.

"No, we were just decorating the tree. What can I do for you?" She dropped onto the bench, since it was quieter in the mud room and the kitchen rang with her sisters' merry and loud chatter.

"It's not what you can do for me, but for our church. And my wife." Steve's jovial tenor sang across the connection. "Laura needs someone to take her place on the Christmas food drive committee. You know she's got her hands full with me. According to her, I'm a terrible patient and I'm a lot of work for her."

"There's no need to talk me into it." Really, as if she could say no. "I'll do it, although I'm stretched thin. I'm kind of afraid to ask how much time it will take."

"Not too much. I'll have Laura email you the info. Thanks, Chelsea. I appreciate it."

"I'm always happy to help you and Laura." Laura had been one of her mom's closest friends. Tears unexpectedly popped into her eyes when she remembered that Mom used to volunteer for the Christmas food drive, too. Her phone beeped. "Sorry, Steve. I have another call coming in."

"Okay. Talk to you soon." The line clicked and he was gone.

"Hello?" she answered the second call and wiped her eyes.

"Dr. McKaslin? This is Janice from the answering service." A polished, professional voice spoke in her ear. "I have a call-back request from Mrs. Wigginsworth. Alicia's fever has returned and is spiking."

So much for cookies and hot chocolate. Chelsea shrugged and made the call.

This was grim news. Very grim news. Michael couldn't get the look on Kelsey's mom's face out of his head as he made his way down the hospital corridor. He punched the elevator call button, hating that the girl had fallen sick, her frantic mother had called him and he'd ordered them to rush straight to emergency. Kelsey's kidney function had taken a bad turn. He winced, his shoulders drooping as he stepped into the elevator. He and a team of specialists had done everything they could, and there was nothing left to do but wait.

The doors opened and he rode the elevator two floors up. On his way down the barren hall, he hauled out his cell and texted his mom. Will B here a while longer. Is that OK?

Macie and I are having great fun, came her reply.
Your father is on his way over.

Thanx. He tucked his phone into his pocket,
turned the corner and stepped into the cafeteria,
his stomach rumbling. He could run home for supper, but leaving the hospital even for a short time
didn't feel right. At least not until more of Kelsey's
test results came in. He grabbed a tray from the
stack and headed straight for the coffee dispenser.

"I heard about Kelsey." Chelsea McKaslin set a
steaming hot cup of water on her tray and chose a
tea bag on the counter.

Why Chelsea? Why did he have to bump into
her of all people? "Kelsey's mom called me directly."

"I know you cover your own patients on off-
hours, but I happened to see them checking in at
the E.R. Judging by the look on your face, things
aren't good."

"They could hardly be worse." He clamped his
molars together, locking his jaw. He didn't want
to talk about it. He had to keep the doors on his
heart closed. He grabbed a cup from the stack
and wedged it beneath the dispenser. "You must
be on call."

"Yes, and I was called in." She balanced the
tray on one slim hip, trying to make eye contact
with him.

As if he was going to let himself be exposed to

the caring in her heartfelt blue eyes, full of under-standing. No way was he going to open that door to his heart, not when he had it locked completely. "Anything serious?"

"A patient had a high temp. She scared us pretty good, but it's on the way down again." She led the way to the refrigerated sandwiches bundled in tidy packages and chose one. "I really dislike antibi-otic resistant bugs."

"Me, too." He might as well take a sandwich too. The turkey and cranberry looked good, so he tossed it onto his tray. "You're still here. Keeping an eye on her?"

"I can't help myself. I'll stay until she's dis-charged, another hour or two." She grabbed a package of chips to add to the sandwich. "Is there anything I can do for Kelsey?"

"I wish." He couldn't look at her. He'd gotten used to handling things on his own, the way he liked it. No way did he want to let anyone in, espe-cially when he had to keep his heart closed. How else would he be able to do his job? "It's wait and see and minimize her symptoms. The lab's run-ning on a skeleton staff."

"Sure, it's the weekend before Christmas." She headed toward the lone cashier. "Waiting is the worst."

"Especially when I want to be able to pre-pare her family for whichever way this goes." He plunked his tray down next to hers, a tall stone statue holding everything in.

"That can't be easy." She watched a muscle tense along his jawline, the only sign he was human and not granite.

"No," he clipped out as the cashier's register beeped. "Some days are worse than others."

Like today, she thought but didn't say it. How many days did he spend like this, fearing for other people's children? The strain showed in the etched lines around his eyes, the furrows in his forehead and the bunched muscles of his jaw.

"I mostly only have to worry about sore throats and earaches and virulent bugs. Maybe stitch up a cut or two." She reached into her pocket for her credit card, but he beat her to it, handing a card to the cashier.

"It's more efficient," he said by way of explanation as the cashier ran it through.

Efficient? She glanced behind them. No one else was in line. There was no need to hurry up, to be efficient, to move on. What did she say to that? "Uh…thanks?"

"Sure. Don't mention it." He shrugged like it was no big deal, avoiding eye contact.

Okay. She grabbed her tray and stepped into the dining area. Mostly empty tables stretched out in a cavernous, echoing room. A few interns sat nearby, fortifying themselves with jumbo cups of coffee and camaraderie. Michael kept at her side as they passed the jovial group. So, did this mean he was going to sit with her, or was he going to go his own way? He nodded toward a secluded table in the corner, framed by windows. Okay, apparently they were going to sit together.

"Did your family find the right Christmas tree?" he asked, sliding his tray on the tabletop.

"Meg spotted it, Sara Beth seconded it and Johanna had a decorating scheme figured out before Dad could flag down one of the dudes with a chainsaw." She set her tray across from his. "It was so big it didn't fit into the back of Dad's truck."

"What did he do?" Michael came over and pulled out her chair for her. Like a gentleman. Or a man who was interested.

Okay, she wasn't expecting that. She sank down in the chair, deciding not to think about it. Maybe Michael was just being polite. Mannerly. Couldn't fault him for that. "Dad had an easy solution. He drove home with the top half of the tree flopping in the wind."

"At least he's trying to make it a normal Christmas." He helped her push in her chair.

"Exactly." She watched him circle around to his chair. "When I left the house, my sisters were decorating the tree. Wait, correct that, they were taking a decorating break that involved sugar and hot chocolate."

"All part of the season." He settled in his chair and folded his hands for grace. "Where was your dad?"

"Out in the barn checking on the horses, or so he said. I just think he needed a breather from it all." She folded her hands, too. "I'm sure he came back smiling and ready to help with the lights. What about your tree?"

"My mother came to the rescue."

"She does that a lot?"

"Constantly. She shores up the crumbling dam that is my attempt at parenthood." Dimples bracketed his shy smile. "I'm not that bad of a father, but I'm not that good. Not by myself, anyway."

"So you're looking for a Mrs.?" Yikes. Her heart thumped wildly in a blinding moment of panic. Did she look like a wife candidate? No. She had a medical practice to build, a shocking school loan to pay off and no time for a husband, not in the near future. No way. But later? Who knew? "A wife?"

"No wife." He shook his head, chuckling. "Marriage was disaster enough the first time around. I'm a smart man. I do my best not to make the same mistake twice."

So relieved to hear it, she thought as the adrenaline kicking through her veins cooled. "I get that. A serious relationship is a slippery slope

I'm in no hurry to climb. Do you want me to say the blessing?"

"Go ahead. I'm ready."

The real challenge was in collecting her thoughts. She still had no reasonable explanation why the man sucked away her common sense like a black hole vacuuming space dust. She wished she wasn't so acutely aware of him. He took up too much space, he was impossible to ignore with his perfect shoulders and stony profile and it really bothered her how she felt comfortable and uneasy with him at the same time.

She bowed her head, doing her best to concentrate. "Dear Father, thank You for this meal. Please help little Alicia to feel better, save Kelsey's kidneys and take extra care of all your children tonight. Above all, we ask that You heal every broken heart and hurting soul You can this Christmas season. Amen."

"Amen," Michael murmured, a shock of sandy-brown hair tumbling over his forehead. His gaze became a sharp, tangible touch on the side of her face.

What was he thinking? It was impossible to tell. Sometimes there were rocks on this planet more expressive than Michael Kramer.

"I hear you and I have something else in common." He took a bite of his sandwich.

"Should I be afraid to ask?" She tore open the chip bag.

"Probably. We have Steve to thank."

"Oh, no. The Christmas food drive." Realization dawned, along with a little panic. She dug a tortilla chip from the bag. "He recruited me today. He knows I can't say no to him and he used it against me. He did it to you too, didn't he?"

"I can't say no to the man, either. It's his favorite charitable project all year long, so I know it has to be tough for him to sit this one out. Steve and his wife oversee the project together. Guess you're taking her place?"

"Apparently, which means we'll be overseeing it together." Wow. Just what she needed. To spend more time trying not to like Michael any more than she already did.

"It's funny how things work out. A few weeks ago, we didn't know one another." He tore open a sugar packet and dumped it into his steaming coffee cup. "Now, I can't seem to get rid of you."

"I know. Crazy, right?" She crunched into another chip, savoring the wonderful crackle. Nothing crunched in a more satisfying way than a tortilla chip. "It's kind of weird, isn't it? I mean, you don't think Steve and Laura would—"

She hesitated because she couldn't make herself say the actual words.

"Set us up?" He stirred his coffee and took a

sip. "No. Steve wouldn't do that. He knows what I went through with Diana. And let's admit it. There are better men for Steve to set you up with."

"I'm glad you see it, too." She gently kidded him and why? Because she knew what happened when he smiled. Yep, the dimples. There they were. Amazing.

"Which brings up a good question." Michael turned in his chair so that he could pin her with his stare. "Why are you still single?"

Chapter Ten

"Wow, how do you want me to answer that?" She quirked one eyebrow at him, cradling her sandwich in both slender hands.

"Did I offend you or something?" It wouldn't surprise him. "I just wondered what was wrong with the men you went to school with? I'm surprised no one snatched you up."

"Don't be." Mischief glinted as she focused her baby blues on him. "I want to be single. I've learned it's easier that way."

"Won't argue there, but you must have done the breaking up. You have heartbreaker written all over you."

"No way." She nibbled at her sandwich, studying him over the bread. "And if I do, it's because I'm focused on my career."

No, it's because you're gorgeous, and he was glad he bit his tongue before he could say it. "Sure.

You work as much as I do. It's tough on a serious relationship."

"I wouldn't know. I broke up with my one and only serious boyfriend back in college." She might think she appeared strong, no scars showing as she reached for a chip, but she would be wrong. "It was senior year, we were both pre-med."

"Let me guess. You were accepted to different med schools?"

"No, we both got in at the University of Washington. That wasn't the problem." She popped a chip in her mouth, chewing, biding time, maybe to figure out how best to answer. "That's when I learned he and I didn't see eye to eye."

"On what, exactly?" Call him curious.

"On what we wanted in life." Locks of light chestnut tumbled over her face like a curtain, hiding her emotions. She dug in the chip bag as if this conversation was no big deal, as if she was over whatever had hurt her. "We were engaged."

He couldn't say why that surprised him. "Wow. Did you have a wedding date set?"

"In August, before med school started." She reached for her teacup, sweet, calm, in control. Only the slight tremble of her hand betrayed her. "Nick wanted me to postpone my studies, find work and put him through school. When he was done, he'd put me through."

"And you didn't go for that?"

"No. He accused me of not loving him enough. That wasn't true, not at all." Her gentle alto cracked. Emotion surfaced, but she visibly forced it back with a bob of her chin. "But when I suggested a compromise, he lost his temper and broke up with me."

"What compromise?"

"That he would be the one to get a job and put me through school first. I mean, shouldn't he have been willing to do that for me, if I had been willing to do it for him?" Sadness rippled across her face and she shrugged it away. Not over her feelings, after all. "He was so angry. Just furious at me. So that's how I found out that he was the one who didn't love me enough."

"I'm sorry you went through that." He set down the remains of his sandwich. She had no idea how sorry. He hated to think of her hurting. "You must have been heartbroken."

"For a long while." She tried to smile but didn't fully succeed. "I'm over it. Life goes on, but it was a good lesson to learn. I'll be careful who I trust my heart and my dreams with next time around."

"Smart." He took another slurp of coffee. She could try to minimize her pain, but he read it in her eyes and felt it in his heart. He didn't want to care so much, he just couldn't help it. "Did he transfer, or did you end up going through the program with him?"

"Oh, no, I saw him regularly. And it wasn't easy, believe me, but Mom and our numerous and long phone calls got me through. I don't know what I would have done without her." She crunched into another chip. "I followed the right dream, the one that wouldn't let me down."

There were so many things he wanted to tell her, like it wasn't her fault the guy had dumped her. It wasn't selfish to put her dreams first. If the man had truly loved her, he'd never have walked away or wanted her to put her goals behind his.

But could he open up like that? He didn't know. He wanted to stay on lockdown because it was better that way so he said the next best thing. "I think life is better when you fill it with more than one dream."

"Did you actually say that, or did I just imagine it?" Mirth brought out violet-blue flecks in her irises, bright with the power to dazzle. "Isn't that a little touchy-feely for a man like you?"

"You're right. I take it back."

"Well, I sort of like it. Sort of. Not much." She studied him through her lashes. "But you're right. You have Macie. You had a marriage. Those are good dreams."

He knew he should say something, he opened his mouth to do it but no words came and no thoughts materialized. The world around him faded, erasing breath by breath, heartbeat by heartbeat until there was only Chelsea, gently luminous and sweet and smart and—

Don't go there, Michael. He shook his head, trying to pull out of the whirlpool that was threatening to suck him down. His phone chimed, saving him. He blinked and his surroundings came back into focus.

"Looks like Kelsey's nephrologist wants to talk test results." He popped the last bite of sandwich into his mouth. "Want to tag along?"

"Like I could say no to that." She popped out of her chair and tugged her tray off the table, ready to go. It was what she didn't say that touched him most—her readiness to help, concern for a sick child and her innate kindness—that got to him.

Don't fall, he told his heart, but did it listen?

Not a chance.

"So, not the very worst news." Kate, Kelsey's mom, hugged herself around the middle, looking frazzled and exhausted and relieved. "As long as we can stave off the very worst, I'm good."

"That's not what I asked." Chelsea leaned against the wall as a gurney ambled by, pushed by an orderly. "How are you really? I've got time. I can run an errand for you. Fetch dinner."

"No, I can't eat." She laid a hand on her stomach. "Although maybe I can in a bit, now that we know Kelsey doesn't need dialysis yet. Yet. She's still with us. Praise God for that. My parents are flying in, they should be landing soon, but thank you."

"I just want to help, remember that, okay?" She liked the woman, who must have been in her early thirties, too. Chelsea thought of the different paths a life could take and wondered what it would be like if she started dreaming other dreams. Not that she was ready for that. "You have my cell, so call if you need it."

"On Sunday? No, I couldn't trouble you." She shook her head, scattering dark hair, her gaze wandering through the doorway and into the room where her daughter lay propped up in bed. "It's your family time."

"I'm on call. It's my job. And I get more than enough time with my family. Too much time, to be honest."

"You're just saying that to make me feel better."

"True, but I'm still going to call you tomorrow and check on you, so be prepared. I don't go away easily." She leaned against the doorjamb, and instead of noticing the adorable child with her arm around a purple bunny, Chelsea's attention zeroed in straight on the quiet, self-contained man in a blue button-down shirt and jeans, giving up his day off to help this family. He spoke with Kelsey's dad, answering questions, his voice too low to hear. She couldn't look away.

"When I first met Michael," Kate began, lowering her voice and pushing a lock of dark hair out of her pale face, "we'd been referred to him by Steve, Kelsey's pediatrician. I'd seen Michael in the office once in the hall when we were in an exam room and he walked by, silent and stonelike, and I wasn't sure he was the right doctor to see us through Kelsey's treatment. I was wrong."

"I'm glad he's here for her." The little girl nodded to something Michael said to her, squeezing her stuffed bunny a little tighter. The trust in the child's eyes said everything she needed to know about him as a doctor and as a man.

"He's a good guy." Realization twinkled in Kate's gaze. "You should give him a chance."

"A chance? You mean, like— No, I'm not interested." Wait, that wasn't true. "I don't want to be interested."

"Sometimes that's the way it goes." Kate stepped into the room.

That's not the way I want it to go, Chelsea wanted to argue, but what was the point? It was time to concede defeat. Her valiant effort not to care for Michael had failed.

Her cell broke into her thoughts. Johanna's message marched across the screen. When R U coming home? We're waiting for U to come so we can put on the balls.

So U got the lights figured out? She tapped in and hit Send.

Yes. Dad took directions very well.

Mom trained him up right, Chelsea quipped, typing away. After she hit Send, she gave Kelsey a finger wave, the parents an encouraging smile and Michael a nod.

"I need to go check on my patient," she explained. "Thanks for dinner."

"Thanks for the company." He paused, as if he wanted to say more, but didn't. Tall, handsome, kind. It was impossible to turn away, but she did it.

"Anytime," she tossed over her shoulder, fighting the terrifying realization that when she walked away, it didn't break the snap of closeness between them. She liked Michael way too much. And not like a coworker, not like a friend, but more.

Much more.

She got Alicia and her mom checked out, tucked safely in their car and headed home through icy roads and darkness. Everywhere she looked shone Christmas cheer in yard displays, house displays and even on her front porch, where garlands of lights hung in the windows to celebrate the season.

"There's my girl." Dad opened the door to welcome her home as Dee barked a greeting. "I heard your boots stomping up the steps. We've been waiting for you."

"Let me take your coat." Meg leaped over to

take the garment Chelsea shrugged out of. "We've got the decorations out of the attic—"

"The ones we could find anyway," Johanna finished, tromping over with a cup of steamy, foamy cocoa. "Here, this will warm you up. I can't believe how cold it is out there."

"Come sit by the fire," Sara Beth invited, patting the cushion of the chair she abandoned. "We'll get you unthawed and then start decorating. Dad, which Christmas album do you want to listen to?"

"It's my pick, is it?" Dad inhaled, as if buoying himself against the painful truth that Mom had always decided the carols they would sing to while they decorated the tree. "Which one did your mother always like?"

"It's by Amy Grant. Let me get it." Sara Beth thumbed through the CDs stored in a drawer, head bent, dark hair tumbling over her slender shoulder. "We'll start with Mom's favorite. That's fitting. Maybe she'll sing along with us as she's looking down from heaven."

"Maybe," Dad said, absently patting the yellow Lab. Dee licked his hand consolingly. "Maybe heaven isn't always so far away."

That was Chelsea's prayer, too. She settled into the chair, careful not to disturb Burt, who snoozed on top of the back cushion, and sipped hot chocolate, thankful to be home with her family. Bayly lifted his head from his dog bed by the hearth, companionably acknowledging her, as they soaked up the heat from the crackling fire together.

"Hey, I got a question for ya." Johanna dropped down on the nearby couch. "Do you remember where we put the special ornaments?"

"The ones Mom got for us every Christmas?" She licked marshmallow fluff off her top lip. "Well, I don't know, not off the top of my head."

"Bummer. They weren't with the regular Christmas stuff in the attic." Johanna plopped her feet on the coffee table and studied her fuzzy slippers. "I thought it might be nice to use them this year. I know we're supposed to keep them for our own families one day, but—" She fell silent.

Chelsea understood exactly what Johanna meant. "If we use them this year, it will be special. A new tradition. Brilliant idea."

"Thanks, I thought so, too."

"I might know where they could be, but don't get your hopes up." She hated leaving the relaxing heat by the fire, but duty called. "Want to come help me look?"

"Just try and stop me." Johanna's feet hit the floor. Bayly sighed and went back to sleep on his comfy bed. "Hey, Meg, keep Dad busy until we get back."

"I'm on it. Holler if you need help." Meg looked up from petting Dee.

"Will do," Johanna promised, leading the way upstairs. "So, we all conferred while you were gone."

"You did? Glad I wasn't there," Chelsea quipped as she went up on tiptoe and yanked down the attic stairs. Cool air radiated from the dark rafters overhead and she climbed up into it. "I hate to ask what you all conferred about."

"Ideas on what to get Dad for Christmas, which came to zip. It's driving me crazy." Johanna flicked on a switch and bare bulbs shot light down from the rafters. "He has everything. He wants nothing. Meg and I have been throwing little hints at him. For weeks. It hasn't done a bit of good."

"What kind of hints?" Chelsea wove around a stack of dusty boxes.

"Like when we're at the clinic and one of us will say, 'Hey, maybe I should spring for a tablet computer like Chelsea has. It's cool, don't you think?' Or 'Do you know what you need? A new saddle,' but we get nothing from him. Not so much as a 'Hmm, that sounds interesting.'"

"A new saddle is a good idea, his is ancient." She ducked, following the slope of the roof. "I can't see him using an iPad. You can barely get him to use the computer."

"Hey, I was desperate. We've tried everything else." Johanna plopped down on an old rocking chair. Dust puffed into the air. "Is it me, or do you seem distracted?"

"I'm not distracted." That wasn't the exact word. Troubled, that was more accurate, troubled and trying to deny it—not that it was working. She picked her way around a little pink bureau that used to be Sara Beth's and opened Mom's old hope chest. "I bumped into Michael Kramer at the hospital this afternoon. He was called in, too."

"That can't be good news, since he's an oncologist." Johanna's forehead furrowed with concern. She was adorable with her thick straight hair, her big brown eyes luminous with concern and her lovely porcelain features. "Did he have to admit a sick child?"

"Yes. A little girl I met at the clinic yesterday. Such a sweetheart. They'd been praying for remission and now her kidneys are in trouble. If she doesn't turn around, the news isn't good." This was the tough side of being a doctor. Everything had two sides—love, life, health. It was the way God had made the world. Nothing on this earth remained, not one thing lasted.

Only love. She pushed aside the tissue paper and a fragile ceramic figurine smiled up at her. An adorable little girl holding a floppy-eared dog. "Found them!"

"Awesome, Chels. You rock." Johanna bolted

out of the chair. "Sara Beth is going to do a Snoopy dance. Using them was her idea. This is just perfect."

"Perfect," Chelsea agreed, holding up the ornament by its delicate gold braid. "I think Mom would approve."

"I do, too." Johanna dropped to her knees and pawed through the tissue paper. "Oh, this is my favorite. A cat with a candy cane. Wait, there's something else here."

"Here, give me the cat." Chelsea took the fragile figurine and set both of them on the floor. "What do you have there?"

"It's a present. A Christmas present." Johanna held the square box the size of a large coffee mug as if she were afraid it would break. "Do you know what this is?"

"No. Let me see." She leaned in to read the foil tag taped neatly beneath the beautiful red crepe ribbon. "To Sara Beth from Mom."

Seeing their mother's handwriting was a shock, as if it was something she could have just written yesterday, as if she wasn't gone after all, as if she could be just downstairs with the rest of the family. Tears burned behind Chelsea's eyes. She sank back on her heels, her knees biting into the rough wood floor.

"She hid it up here, like she always did. Remember how she'd start Christmas shopping in

January?" Johanna laid the wrapped box down shakily. "She was hoping to be here for one more Christmas."

"We were hoping, too." Their mom had left one final gift, one that meant more than any other. "We have to tell Sara Beth."

"Wait, there's more." Johanna pawed out another identical box wrapped in festive Christmas paper and tied with a fancy bow. "To Meg. Oh, and this is for me. Chels, there's one more in here."

Chelsea closed her eyes, listening to the crackle of tissue paper. She didn't think she could bear it, this last present from Mom. When she opened her eyes, Johanna held out the last box, wrapped in cheerful red paper and topped with a silver bow.

To my Chelsea, she read on the tag, taking the gift with an unsteady hand. *With all my love, Mom.*

The words blurred with the tears she held back. Memories rushed in and pushed away all her sadness. Of Mom standing in the corner of the attic, a scarf wrapped around her head, searching for the angel topper for the tree. Of Mom's melodic alto rising and falling with a Christmas carol's tune as she wrapped presents at the kitchen table. Of Mom stashing gifts in the back of the hallway closet. "Oops, Chelsea, there you are. Whatever you do, don't tell your sisters I stash presents in here."

Chelsea blinked to keep tears from falling as the memories faded. The attic came into clear focus around her with its mishmash of stacked stuff and Johanna on her knees, her hands to her face. Her poor little sister. "Hey, are you okay?"

"Sure. Yeah. Fine." After a muffled sniff Johanna lowered her hands, trying to dismiss her true feelings with a shoulder shrug. "It just took me by surprise, that's all. Just thinking of Mom hiding these when she was so sick, and I was—" Johanna's sob echoed against the open beams and she lowered her face into her hands again.

"I know." Chelsea scooted over to slip an arm around her sister. "I miss her so much I can't breathe."

"Me, too." Johanna leaned in, resting her head on Chelsea's shoulder. When sisters were together, everything was a little easier. "I just wish we could roll back time, just once, to see her again. Just for a one day."

"Any day," Chelsea agreed. "A day with Mom in it was a good day."

"Remember her laugh?" Johanna rubbed her wet cheeks with her sleeve. "And how she was always singing? I'm not sure one day would be enough. If my wish could come true, if God did turn back time, I'd still want another day with her."

"Me, too." Chelsea spotted the edge of another figurine in the crinkled paper and unearthed it. She held up the ornament by its gold braid, four little girl angels singing. "Her love is still here."

"It really is." One last tear trailed down Johanna's cheek. "Do you hear that? Mom's favorite song."

It drifted up from the stairwell, Dad, Meg and Sara Beth's voices singing in harmony. The thing about life was that it whizzed by so fast with responsibilities and things to get done and to-do lists to complete that it was easy to forget every passing moment was golden. Once spent, it was gone forever. It mattered how you spent it.

"C'mon." Chelsea held out her hand. "Let's take this stuff down. We've got a tree to decorate."

"And songs to sing," Johanna finished, smiling through watery eyes. "And cookies to eat."

"And hot chocolate to drink." Her blessings were all around her in the family she loved. A bright flash at the far side of the attic grabbed her attention. The icicle lights, dangled in front of the single round window, dancing in the night breeze as if moved by a loving hand. Chelsea adored those lights. Somehow Mom didn't feel far away.

She scooped up the ornaments, Johanna gathered the presents and they headed downstairs together.

Chapter Eleven

God graced the day with flawless sun and sky, which framed the white steeple church on Mission Street with heavenly beauty. At the base of the wide cement stairs, Michael hugged his little girl in the after-service rush, not wanting to let her go. Kelsey's condition weighed heavy on his heart as he knelt in front of his Macie, the daughter he loved. "I'll be home soon and we'll do something fun."

"Like going sleighing?" Bluebonnet blue eyes pinched with the power of her plea.

"Sure, okay, we can go sledding. I'll dig out your sled from the garage—"

"No. *Sleighing*. Like at the stables. Remember, I told you?" She shook her head at him, tsking like a schoolmarm, her brown curls a soft cloud around her face. Nothing on earth could be cuter. "A horse and sleigh. Like the song, 'Jingle Bells'? Do I have to sing it for you, Daddy?"

"No, I get it." He tweaked her nose. "I know the song. I was thinking more along the lines of putting up lights on the house."

"Really? Did you hear that, Grammy? He didn't say no." Macie tilted her head, gazing up at her grandmother expecting complete solidarity.

"I stand as witness. I heard no 'no.' You're in trouble now, son." Mom caught Macie's gloved hand. "Call if you're going to be late."

"I'll keep you updated," he promised.

"See you later, alligator." Macie tromped off beside her grandmother heading for the parking lot while chatting away, his precious girl.

"What a sweetheart." A woman's voice caught his attention, but he didn't recognize her until she was at his side. Mrs. Collins. "Looks like the McKaslin girls underreported things. My kittens won't be going to a good home. They'll be going to a great one. Your daughter is so sweet and gentle. It's easy to see those little ones will be well loved."

"Big-time. I can promise you."

"Say, Dr. Steve said you were taking his place on the food drive committee. We're a small group, but vital. It's hard to think we have families in our own church struggling to put food on the table. I think we are going to make this the best food drive in our history."

"Sounds like a noble goal." He thought of the families he knew, struggling to pay medical costs and hold on to their homes, and the ones he didn't, drowning in these uncertain economic times. "Glad to help. Should we head inside and get started?"

"We have a few minutes yet. I've got a few people to chat up and then I'll be in." She secured the ends of her scarf more tightly beneath her chin and hurried off, waving down the choir director.

His phone buzzed as he climbed the church steps, going against the grain. The last of the churchgoers straggled out as he shouldered in. Warmth enveloped him as he crossed the vestibule, the coved ceiling overhead echoing with his footsteps. He wove around the food donation barrels. The wide double doors leading into the sanctuary stood open and gave him a perfect view of a woman kneeling, her light chestnut locks cascading down her back and her head bowed in prayer.

Chelsea. The sun through the stained glass windows found her, washing her with jewel colors of light. He'd never seen anyone so beautiful.

"Michael." She rose from the pew, gathering her wool coat and bag from the seat. "I figured I'd be running into you here."

"Imagine that." A smile broke through him like the first rays of morning sun, and he didn't like it. He didn't like the change in him because of her. "Guess we have a meeting to attend. Hope it doesn't take long. I haven't had lunch yet."

"Me either. My stomach is rumbling." She swished into the aisle, her sapphire blue dress nipping in at her small waist and swirling around her knees. "I was just saying a prayer for Kelsey and her family."

"I'm sure they would appreciate that." The Koffmans hadn't shown up for church, not wanting to leave their daughter's side. Every moment they spent with Kelsey was precious, and time was ticking down. At least, that was his fear. "No calls, so Kelsey's holding steady."

"That's what her mom said in her text this morning." Chelsea folded her coat and slung it across her slender arm. "I checked in on her, I promised to keep in touch. Maybe there's something I can do to help, even if it's running errands or bringing them a meal."

"That's beyond the call of duty." He ambled closer. Chelsea's ability to care about others was one thing he admired about her. "It's nice of you."

"No, it's the season." She dismissed his compliment with a wave of her slim hand. "I'm in the Christmas spirit. It's really why we're here on this earth. To help one another."

"Can't argue with that." Or the fact that he'd fallen for her, hard and fast. He had no idea what to do about it, so he shuffled his feet, staring down at the polished toes of his shoes. Before he could say anything more, footsteps tapped in the aisle behind him.

"So, the rumors are true. Michael, you *are* here." Dr. Susan Benedict rushed down the aisle. "Steven told me, but I didn't believe it. I'm so glad you're taking his place."

"Steve is hard to say no to." Grateful for the interruption, he tried to pry his attention away from Chelsea beside him.

No good. No matter how hard he tried, Chelsea stayed in his periphery, not his focus, as she marched to a stop.

"That's why I'm here, too," Chelsea's soft alto warmed with humor, drawing him in, holding him captive. She greeted Susan with a smile. "The inability to say no."

"Tell me about it. I fell into that trap years ago," Susan admitted, her voice distant to his ears when Chelsea's was not.

As the women chatted and Mrs. Collins joined them, all he could see was Chelsea. Chelsea smiling. Chelsea laughing. Chelsea's interest as she asked about the kittens. Watching her, he felt a door open to his heart. He couldn't do a thing to stop it.

Okay, so this isn't so bad, right? Chelsea thought as she scooted her chair closer to the table in the minister's cozy kitchen. *I'm well fed and warm,*

I'm in good company and this apple cobbler is to die for. Everything's good. Well, except for one thing.

The man across the table. Michael's resonant voice rumbled in answer to the minister's question and everyone else around the table nodded, so she did, too. Could she concentrate? No. Her mind whirled way too much for that, going around and around on an endless loop. Every time she glanced at him her feelings grew. She felt a sparkle, like twinkle lights on a Christmas tree, festive and bright and hopeful.

This wasn't good. Not good at all.

"Chelsea and I will do it." Susan spoke up beside her, looking at her expectantly. "It'll be fun, right?"

"Uh, sure. Right." Warning bells went off in her head. Maybe she hadn't been as subtle about gaping at Michael as she'd thought. And really, she should be paying better attention. Well, whatever she'd volunteered to do would be more fun with Susan. "Okay."

"Great. I think you two ladies will work well together. We already have a large portion of our pledged funds from local business owners." Paul, the minister, nodded his approval. "It will take a few phone calls and time to pick up donations. I'll leave you two to coordinate that. Michael will work with Mrs. Collins on our list of our church families in need. Things are going right on schedule."

"Excellent. It sounds like your meeting is over." Amy, the minister's wife, sauntered over with a teapot in hand. "Anyone want a refill?"

"Not for me, thanks." Michael stood, all six feet plus of him towering over the table. "I need to get home to my daughter."

Don't look at him, don't notice him, don't do it, Chelsea. She fixed her eyes firmly to the dregs at the bottom of her teacup and declined Amy's offer of a refill.

"I love how Macie decorated her cast, so creative." Amy moved on to her husband's cup and poured. "All those stickers."

"They came from Chelsea." His tone warmed like melted chocolate when he said her name. Or was it her imagination?

"Actually, I can't take credit. They came from Johanna," Chelsea explained, ready to leave, but timing was everything. If she stood to leave at this exact moment, she'd wind up walking out with Michael. Not so good, considering how hard she'd been fighting to hide her growing feelings all meeting long. Which was totally exhausting, by the way. What she needed was serious non-Michael time to get her head on straight, her feelings in order and figure out what to do because the man was driving her crazy.

When she felt his gaze on her face like a touch, she resisted. She did not look up.

"Johanna." Amy smiled fondly. "Giving out stickers sounds like her. She's generous to a fault. Such a lovely soprano. Speaking of which, guess I'll see you and Susan tomorrow evening. Ensemble practice."

"We'll be there," Susan reassured, but all Chelsea could do was listen to the drum of Michael's footsteps on the linoleum floor. The slight squeak of the hinges opening and the bite of cold wind sailing through the door told her he was almost out of range. Just a few more seconds, he'd be totally gone and everything would go back to normal.

"Guess we'll be going, too." Susan stood, catching Chelsea's elbow and tugging.

"I guess so." She reluctantly stood, unable to think of a logical reason why she couldn't—or one she could admit to.

"We'll leave you two to your Sunday afternoon," Susan said to the minister and his wife as she shrugged into her coat. "I've got grocery shopping to do if I want to eat tonight. Amy, lunch was delicious."

"Yes, very delicious," Chelsea agreed, lifting her coat from the coat tree. "Thanks again."

"My pleasure. You both have a nice afternoon." Amy waved them off and closed the door.

Breathing in the frosty air, Chelsea wrapped her

scarf around her neck. Michael was a dark figure against the stretch of white that was the lawn. The sun shone so bright it hurt her eyes, the day was crystal clear. That was Michael's effect, he was doing this to her. The last time she'd felt this way, it ended with disaster.

"I was right, wasn't I?" Susan asked, the heels of her boots crunching on the icy walkway. "You seriously like him."

"And trying not to." She yanked on her mittens, which gave her something to look at aside from the man. "I'm sure it's something passing. You know, like a virus. It strikes but you eventually fight it off."

"It could be like that," Susan agreed amiably. "Or it could be more serious. An advanced infection you can't get rid of."

"One resistant to antibiotics?"

"And there's no getting rid of it," Susan confirmed.

"I hope it's not like that." Chelsea forced her gaze to the ice in front of her shoes but she could see Michael at the edge of her vision. He'd reached his shiny SUV and beeped open his locks. His gaze found hers and her pulse lurched crazily. One foot missed the concrete walkway and she plunged into deep snow. Cold seeped through her tights.

Great going, Chelsea, just brilliant. She pulled her foot out of the snow, hoping no one else noticed. What if this emotional condition she felt for Michael wasn't temporary? "Hey, if it is like that with Michael, I'm here for consultation." Susan smiled, her soft curls dancing in the breeze. "Maybe we can brainstorm a treatment plan."

"I appreciate the offer."

"No problem. I'm jazzed because I think we're going to be good friends."

"Me, too." Now *that* was something to smile about. "What's up for your afternoon, other than grocery shopping?"

"I have presents to wrap so I can get them in tomorrow's mail." Susan headed toward her gleaming SUV. "Time is running out. Christmas will be here before we know it."

"No kidding." Time kept ticking down, she knew of no way to stop it. She pulled her key chain out of her pocket. "Have fun wrapping. I'll see you Monday."

"Count on it. Plus we have our food drive stuff to coordinate. Should be fun." Susan opened her Jeep's door.

"I'll put it on my list." She dug out her keys, standing next to her poor old Toyota. "See you."

"Bye." Susan waved, ducked into her vehicle and closed the door. A second later her engine roared to life.

Okay, she should be minding her own business, but as she yanked open her car door she caught sight of Michael again. He sat behind the wheel of his SUV, talking on the phone as he let his engine warm.

She dropped into her front seat, wishing she didn't care about him so much. Fine, she could admit it. She couldn't stop her feelings, but they were a one-way street. Michael had never given her a single reason to think that he cared about her in the same way. Look on the bright side. It wasn't as if she was in mortal danger of falling into a relationship. No need to panic.

Chelsea plugged in her key and gave it a little gas. The engine rolled over and over but didn't spark.

Uh-oh. She said a prayer and tried again. Success. The engine coughed to life, cold air shot out of the vents, and she pulled her iPad out of her purse and studied her screen.

Church meeting. Check. She'd head home, change out of her church clothes and what was up next? *Christmas shopping.* She had a different list for that. While she tapped on the screen to pull it up, Michael's vehicle motored away. If only he didn't take her heart with him, she thought. If only.

If only he could get the pictures of her out of his head, Michael thought, as well as his feelings for her from his heart. He pulled into his driveway and parked next to his mom's van. His air rose in white puffs as he headed for the door. Every step he took was haunted by the memory of Chelsea standing in the parking lot awash in sunlight. Of how animated and lovely she'd been as she spoke with Susan and later settled behind her steering wheel with her tablet computer screen shining softly on her heart-shaped face.

It wasn't the images of Chelsea that were the biggest problem, but the warm affection that had slipped in. An unseen glow gathered behind his ribs and refused to budge. This was a very treacherous change of events. It was one thing to like the woman, but another to truly care. Not sure what the solution was, he took a moment to check the to-do list on his phone, sorted through his key ring and headed for the porch.

"Michael." The door swung open before he could insert the key. Mom stood in the entry in a cabled sweater and jeans, her salt and pepper hair tied back in a ponytail. "Look what the wind blew in, Macie."

"Daddy!" She skipped across the living room. "Grammy and I were defending our castle."

"You were?" He elbowed the door shut. He didn't know what to do with such a fanciful child. "You built a castle? In the living room?"

"In the dining room." She skidded to a stop in front of him and gave him a hug. Sweet, sweet. His heart skipped a beat as he held her for a precious moment before she bounced away. "You gotta come see. Grammy is the captain of the guard. She protects the princess."

"Is that right?" He shrugged out of his coat and arched an eyebrow at his mom in question, but she seemed to understand things he couldn't. Make-believe came easily to her. Maybe he could clarify things. "I didn't know a girl could be captain of the guard."

"Dad, what am I going to do with you?" Macie grabbed him by the hand and dragged him into the dining room. "Girls can do anything."

"Right. I knew that." He was out of his depth in this girl world. Flowered pink sheets were draped over the dining room table—minus the chairs—and tied back at the front with pink hair ribbons as a sort of door. Beneath the table was a fleece blanket spread out like a carpet, throw pillows from the family room sectional and luncheon plate sporting a few of Mom's Christmas cookies. "Looks like you two girls were having fun."

"We were celebrating," Mom explained as she grabbed a broom leaning against the wall. "We just defeated the evil trolls."

"We vanquished them," Macie declared, gesturing toward the Swiffer leaning upright in the corner. Perhaps the other weapon?

"Congratulations. Am I supposed to help with the trolls?" He stood there totally stumped.

"Nope, the trolls have returned to their lair," Macie explained, her cheeks flushed pink with pleasure. "But tomorrow they will be back with another plan to kidnap the princess."

"After school, I hope," he added.

"And the captain of the guard and I will be ready, right, Grammy?"

"Right," Mom asserted with a nod. "Well, now that the enemies have retreated for the day, I'd best get home. Michael, I left the information from the stable right by the phone."

"Uh, thanks?"

"The phone number's there, too. I talked with Natalie. She's the driver." Mom sailed through the living room, calling out of sight. "Just leave the tent, Mace. No need to put it away. We'll just have to haul everything out tomorrow."

"Mom?" He heard the rustle of her coat and the jingle of her keys. His stomach gripped with foreboding. "Don't tell me you—"

"Yes, I did. You can thank me later." The door swished open. "I had to do something. You do not take enough time to relax, my boy. Have a good time."

"I salute you, Captain of the Guard!" Macie called out, hand held to her forehead like a soldier.

"I salute you, Princess Macie. See you tomorrow, sweetheart." The door closed and Mom was gone, leaving him alone with her nefarious plan.

"She reserved a sleigh and driver, didn't she?" he asked his daughter.

"Well, you didn't say no, Daddy."

"My fault entirely. I see that now." Life with his daughter was amazing. "Guess that means we have no other choice. We have to go on this sleigh ride."

"Good, cuz I want to a lot." She patted her cast. "A *lot*."

"So I've heard." He ruffled her hair, brown locks baby-soft against his fingertips. He loved his girl. "Let's go see what notes your grammy left me."

"Okay. Do you wanna cookie?" She ducked into her castle to fetch the waiting plate.

"No, I'm good." He headed through the archway into the kitchen, which was ablaze with decorations. There was a reasonable chance they may have overdone it with the lights yesterday. Twinkle sets were strung from the curtain rods and flashed along the top of the kitchen cabinets. It did feel festive, and it made Macie happy. That was all that mattered.

He found his mother's note on the message pad by the phone. "Call Natalie," his mother's writing scrawled across the page. "She's waiting. Try to have fun for a change, Michael."

"Hey, I'm a fun guy," he said to himself, even if he was sure it wasn't entirely true.

Maybe it was time to turn that around, he thought, reaching for the phone, and his decision wasn't based on the thought of Chelsea McKaslin smiling at him in church, awash in jeweled light.

Chapter Twelve

"New halter for Sara Beth's gift." Check. Chelsea pulled her tablet computer out of her bag and squinted at the screen in the afternoon sun. *"New e-reader cover for Meg."* Check. That meant she only had Johanna's gift left to get.

Oh, and Dad. The man was impossible to shop for. She tucked her iPad into her bag and squinted in the shop's festive front window and considered the hand-tooled leather saddle on display. Dad could use a new saddle, but it just didn't feel right. She bit her bottom lip, debating. No, she'd keep thinking. She still had a week to go before Christmas.

Her cell chimed. When she dug it out, she found a text from Sara Beth. Since UR out and about, pick up milk for supper, OK?

OK. She figured it couldn't hurt to do it next and

get it over with. She hit Send, tucked her phone into her pocket and eyed her car.

The poor, ancient sedan looked dated and tired wedged between a shiny black Navigator and a polished BMW. But she loved her car. She fished for her keys, remembering the days when the four of them crammed in the backseat singing "We Wish You A Merry Christmas" while Mom tried a third time to parallel park. Smiling to herself, she unlocked the door, plopped onto the seat and turned the key.

The engine didn't roll over. It didn't even try. Just a click, that was it and nothing. Absolutely, positively nothing.

No! She grabbed the steering wheel and gave it a shake, as if that would make a difference. "C'mon, car. You have to start. You can do it, right?"

Not surprisingly, the sedan didn't answer. But that didn't stop her from turning the key again, praying for a different outcome even as she heard the click and silence.

This can't be good, she thought, yanking out her key and whipping open the door. Icy air bathed her face as she hopped to her feet. Okay, she was clueless here, not being a mechanic. What could she do? Open the hood and try to look and see if something obvious had fallen apart?

Traffic ambled by on the street, shoppers trudged by on the sidewalk and she leaned against the front fender, dug for her phone and hoped whatever was wrong wouldn't be expensive. The tiny cushion on her credit card had taken a hit from Christmas shopping.

"Chelsea!" A little girl's voice rang above a silvery jingle on the road. Two horses swept by in the lane, pulling a two seat sleigh.

"Whoa!" the driver—Natalie from the stables—called out, steering into an open delivery space along the curb. The horses chomped at their bits, their breaths rising in great white clouds. "Hi, Chelsea."

"Hi, Nat." She shoved off her car. "Macie, you look like a princess in there."

"I know." The girl leaned over the side of the sleigh, adorable in her pink coat, purple hat and scarf. Her eyes shined. "We're out for a country drive."

"So I see." She bit her bottom lip, not pointing out there was no country in sight since they were on a side street in town. Over the top of Macie's head, she spotted Michael Kramer watching her with cool, guarded eyes. "Don't tell me if she's a princess, that makes you the king?"

"Believe me, I was uncomfortable with it." Humility looked good on him, too. "I talked her into being the royal physician instead."

"Much more fitting, although still a little exalted for the likes of you," she quipped.

"Tell me about it, but it's the best I could do." Laughter looked good on him, too. "Having car trouble? Don't try to deny it. I saw the whole thing."

"It's nothing. Let me rephrase that. I'm hoping it's nothing." None of this was Michael's problem and he didn't need to hear about it. Besides, she didn't want to open up to him that much. Considering her feelings for him, it would be much better if he gave Natalie the go ahead to send the horses galloping. But did she? Not a chance. "So, tell me, Macie, how did you talk your solemn father into a jingle bell sleigh ride?"

"Me and my grammy ganged up on him." Macie's honesty was precious and so was the head tilt that sent her soft brown curls swinging. "Plus, I really, really like horses. I've only been taking lessons since school started, but you know what?"

"What?" She leaned in when every instinct she had shouted, run, run, run.

"After a whole year of lessons, that's when I can get my very own horse. I can't wait. I love riding, and this isn't the same, but it's with a horse. Two horses," she corrected, talking fast, so excited. "It's really fun, too."

"I know, my family used to go on sleigh rides. Once. Long ago." She patted the girl's gloved hand, that was clutching the side of the sleigh.

"You have a fun time, Princess Macie. I feel like I should curtsy."

"Chelsea." Michael leaned across his daughter, his eyes an unreadable blue shield. "Do you need a lift? We can take you wherever you need to go."

"That's nice, but what I need is a tow truck."

"It's the Sunday before Christmas. That might take a while, if it even comes." He held out his gloved hand, palm up, his gaze a steady light guiding her closer.

Why did she lay her hand on his? No idea. No rational explanation came to mind but if one had, it would have been blown into bits by the zing of emotion that radiated from his touch and into the depths of her heart. It felt right, meant to be, a force impossible to stop as she settled onto the seat beside him. Was she even breathing?

"You can be my best friend." Macie's declaration rose above the chime of the bells as the horses launched into motion down the compact snow-and-ice street. "Princess Chelsea."

"I've never been a princess before," she admitted. "Not sure I'm princess quality."

"You absolutely are." Michael's baritone rumbled over her, deep and resonant and as familiar as if she'd been listening to it her entire life. He whipped out his cell and tapped in a text with an industrious bend of his head. Probably work related.

"Chelsea, you live in the kingdom next door,"

Macie explained, the pom-pom on top of her knit hat bobbing up and down as she bounced, her enthusiasm too great to be contained. "We could be neighbors."

"Cool." Her make-believe skills might be rusty, but that didn't stop her from joining in. "It was very nice of you to drive all this way to pick me up, Princess Macie."

"It's my pleasure, Princess Chelsea." Macie settled herself regally on the seat. "Welcome to the royal carriage."

"Yes, welcome." Michael's hand caught hers, helping her into the sleigh and onto the seat beside him.

"Thanks." Try to ignore the steely, masculine arm pressed against hers, she told herself. But the more she tried, the more aware of him she became. Aware of the strength of his muscles, the tractor beam of his presence and the fact that they were breathing in synchrony. The white clouds of breath wafted upward in irrefutable proof.

Maybe she'd better think of something other than Michael. The sleigh, the driver, the horses—anything would be a better topic. "Uh—this is a great way to travel. Macie, I love the jingle bells."

"They are royal jingle bells. Very special." Macie lowered her chin with a slow, dignified dip to equal any queen's. "Do you know what? We're going on an adventure."

"Awesome. I love adventures. Especially if they are well planned out. I like to plan." Maybe it was time to remind herself of that. Big time. "I'm a stick-to-the-plans kind of girl."

"Oh, I've got it all figured out." Macie swung her booted feet. "We're going to the far glaciers to see wild polar bears."

"Really? I should have brought my warmer coat."

"And when we're done, we're coming back for tea and cookies." Macie leaned back against the seat. "Then Dad is gonna put up the lights."

"Sounds like a very g-good plan to me." Her words came out shaky, as if the sleigh were bouncing over ruts in the road. Except there were no ruts. And it was all Michael's fault. She knew just who to blame, especially since his arm pressed against hers with such force she could hardly think. *Don't think about him, think about Macie's imaginary adventure.* "I'm not sure I want to see polar bears. They might be hungry, see us and think, great. Supper."

"Nope. My servants put a bag of polar bear food in the back." Macie nodded confidently. "We'll be safe."

"Do you know the best way to keep polar b-bears from h-hunting you?" Chelsea's teeth started chattering and she wished it was because of the biting cold wind. She really, really did. She felt Michael shift on the seat beside her, drawing her thoughts away from polar bears. *Focus, Chelsea.* "Singing soothes them. They particularly like Christmas carols."

"Really? Like which ones?" This was apparently news to Macie. "Like 'Jingle Bells'?"

"Especially 'Jingle B-bells.'" Boy, were her teeth really chattering. She clenched her molars together and yet all they did was rattle. "D-dashing thr-rough the sn-snow—"

"You seem to be cold." Michael spoke low against her ear.

"I'm f-fine," she stuttered.

"—in a one-horse soapin' sleigh—" Macie chimed sweetly.

"It's open sleigh," Chelsea leaned over to whisper and that's when it happened. Michael's arm slid around her shoulders, capturing her, holding her close.

"Maybe this will help." He tucked her against his side.

Help? How was this helping? He was warm and cozy, like a crackling hearth on a winter's day, and solid just the way a dream man should be.

"—over the fields we go," Macie sang. "Laughing all the way."

"Isn't this a little cozy for us, since we're co-workers?" she whispered because her larynx had decided to stop working properly. Call an otolaryngologist. "I mean it's a little snug."

"True, but it's cold outside." Unperturbed, his arm remained hooked around her shoulders. She could feel the intake of his breath, which continued to match hers.

"Bells on bobtowers ring—" Macie continued on, adorably oblivious that the word was *bobtail*. "Making spirits bright—"

My spirit is very bright, Chelsea thought, and outshining the sun, even if that sun was drifting behind swift moving clouds. If only she could stop leaning into him, but she couldn't. She relaxed, letting go, simply savoring the moment of feeling safe and protected. Being with him was, well, amazing.

"What fun it is to ride and sing a sleighing song tonight," Macie belted out. Airy snowflakes began to fall like pieces of heavenly grace.

"Oh, jingle bells…" Michael's baritone rumbled through her, as if the words were hers, as if spoken with her breath. She'd never felt so close to anyone before.

"J-jingle b-bells," she tried to sing but all she could see was Michael. Michael and his kindness, Michael and his strength, Michael the man she l—

No, not the "L" word! she told herself firmly. Absolutely not. That one life-changing word was totally not allowed. Completely off-limits. Banished from her thoughts in regards to Michael forevermore.

"Jingle all the way." Macie snuggled up on Chelsea's other side as the sleigh left the town behind. Their three voices, baritone, alto and soprano, rose on a gust of wind, as snowflakes caught on their eyelashes. Macie finished up the song. "…in a one horse soapin' sleigh."

"Bravo." Chelsea clapped her mitten hands. "Excellent. We could go on the road."

"We *are* on a road," Macie pointed out.

"As a band." Michael laughed. Chelsea's merriment was infectious and it seeped into him strong enough to drive out the cold.

"I'm not so sure about your dad." She eyed him dubiously. "Can you see him onstage?"

Macie furrowed her brow, studying him carefully. "Nope."

"Me, either," Chelsea agreed. "That means it'll be just the two of us, Macie. You and me on tour, garnering recognition and fame."

"The Two Princesses," he offered. Not that he was given to whimsy, but he could play along. "Maybe you two don't have to shut me out completely. I could be your manager."

"No, I think we could do better," Chelsea quipped, so darling with her pink cheeks from the wind and snowflakes dotting her hair like glitter. Never had he seen anyone more incredible. His arm tightened around her just a little, drawing her closer against him just an inch more. Could she tell? Had he revealed his feelings?

"But you could still be my dad," Macie informed him, cute as a button.

"Thanks, baby." Something strange was happening to him, something he couldn't stop. Because of Chelsea tucked against him, slight and sweet, affection crept through his chest, starting with a pure white glow and building until it was all he could feel.

"We wish you a merry Christmas—" Chelsea began in her dulcet alto.

Macie took up the second line and belted it out like a pro. The two females sang above the constant, joyous ring of the sleigh bells as the Wyoming countryside flew by. Sprawling white fields, the golden light of an occasional house looking cozy in the snowfall and the endless white veil reaching from earth all the way to heaven.

He couldn't think of a better way to spend the afternoon as he joined in singing.

Well, it was tough to ignore his arm around her, Chelsea thought as the sleigh came to a stop in the snowy field next to the riding stable's parking lot. Very tough, indeed. And it was nearly impossible not to read anything into the gesture, especially since he didn't move away. They sat there, cuddled together in the falling snow as Macie bounced to her feet.

"See? I told you, Macie." Natalie set down her reins. "Big-time fun, right?"

"Right!" The girl hopped to the ground with a two-footed landing. "My favorite part was the penguins."

"True, but it was a good thing the polar bears didn't try to catch us for dinner," Natalie gamely answered, climbing down, too.

There was nothing else to do. Time to get up and move away from Michael. Chelsea leaned forward, found her feet and shoved off the seat. His warmth seemed to cling to her as she landed in the snow behind Macie, who was retelling their adventure in the wilds of the Arctic as princesses (and their personal doctor) while Natalie listened raptly.

"She's so cute," Natalie mouthed.

Chelsea nodded. No argument there. Michael came up beside her and settled his hand on Macie's shoulder.

"C'mon, let's trek to the car, cutie." He gently steered her toward the parking lot and the SUV lightly draped in white. "Chelsea, we'll take you home."

"No, that's all right." Warning bells sounded in her head. She wanted to be near to him, to hear the warmth knell in his voice, to admire the lean lines of his chiseled face, to be snuggled close to him once again with his comfort surrounding her—Oops, now the alarm bells were clanging louder. "I'll call home. Someone will come pick me up."

"No need. We can take you." He casually pulled his keys from his pocket.

"No, that's too much tr-trouble." There she went, stuttering again. The man simply overwhelmed her. "Besides, I need to call a tow truck."

"It's already done."

"What?" Her foot sank into a sinkhole in the snow and his gloved hand closed around her elbow, catching her, keeping her steady, not letting her fall. *What about your plan, Chelsea? Remember your no-man plan? Five years, career, no man. Not one. Not even this one. Especially not this one.*

"I texted a former patient's father. He runs a garage in town." Michael escorted her to his SUV. "He's probably sent you a text. Get in, you can come with us."

"She can sit in back with me, Daddy," Macie offered, bounding over.

"No, she's sitting up front with me." He swung open the door for her.

Chelsea fumbled onto the seat, numb from what surely was not the cold temperature of the day. What was wrong with her? She couldn't blink, she wasn't sure she could breathe. She listened to him close her door and open Macie's. She couldn't move a single muscle. Not even an eyelid. Dazed, that's what this was. Overwhelmed by the man.

"Do you know what?" Macie asked as she struggled to buckle her seat belt. "Dad's gonna put up the lights next."

"You mean you haven't got them up yet?" Chelsea caught Michael's grimace in the side mirror. "Slacker."

"Can't deny it." He shut his daughter's door, effectively ending the conversation. He picked it up again after he dropped behind the steering wheel. "Between one thing and another, I haven't had the chance."

"Excuses, excuses."

"Tell me about it." He turned the key, the engine purred to a start and his gaze held hers.

In those icy-blue depths she thought she saw a spark of caring and affection, but it disappeared in a blink. Had she imagined it, or had it been real? How could she be sure it wasn't just wishful thinking? And the fact that she was wishing was a shocker.

"It's time. No more excuses." He turned on the wipers and they swished powdered snow off the windshield. "This afternoon it is. I've already honed my skills helping with your family's lights, so I'm good to go. I can whip them up, no problem, especially if I have an assistant."

"Macie?" Chelsea arched a slim brow at him. "That doesn't sound like a good idea. Isn't she really young for that?"

"I was thinking about you." The words popped out, blithely and casually, as if this wasn't the biggest mistake he'd made in years. He should be panicking.

"Me? Why me?" Amusement played in the corners of her pretty mouth. "What did I do to deserve that?"

"I'll never tell." Taking her home should be his first priority, but what did he do? At the end of the stable's long driveway he turned left heading home instead of right toward hers.

"Really, Daddy?" Macie's voice rose higher, full of joy. "Chelsea's really comin' home with us? You've got to see my room and our Christmas tree and Grammy picked me up some stickers. I don't have an awesome collection, but I have some glittery ones."

"That sounds like fun. You know I love stickers."

"I do," Macie nodded emphatically.

Chelsea. Why she affected his heart remained a mystery. But it happened every time he was near her. The flying snow shined neon white and the wintry world appeared so blindingly perfect he wondered why he hadn't noticed before. It was like suddenly putting on a pair of rose-colored glasses.

Chelsea was doing this to him. Letting this happen was a mistake, but the thought of turning around and taking her home and saying goodbye to her— no, that was one thing he wanted to put off as long as possible. He arched one brow instead. "I hear you're good with a ladder."

"You heard wrong, buster. Really, I'm a better supervisor. You know, from the ground. Calling out orders to the grunt on the rungs?" Mirth made her eyes more violet than blue. Stunning.

Keep your gaze on the road, not on the woman. "Sorry, I don't need a supervisor. I'm looking for an equal partner. Someone to climb up with me. Fair is fair. I assisted you, now you assist me."

"No good deed goes unpunished?"

"I wouldn't say this is punishment exactly. It's the Christmas season. It's time for good deeds."

"And for miracles." She leaned back against the leather seat, looking like a miracle of goodness and beauty. "Good thing for you, I'm in a Christmas mood."

"Me, too." The words slipped out, true and straight from his soul. His mood *did* seem bright, brighter than ever, as he steered the SUV around a sweeping corner, taking them home.

Chapter Thirteen

Chelsea glanced down the residential street, not surprised by the beautiful new homes decked with good cheer and Christmas decorations. "I don't even have to ask which house is yours."

"No lights. It's a dead giveaway."

"No kidding." Every other house glowed and gleamed except for a dark shadowy structure at the end of the cul-de-sac. He wheeled into the driveway and hit the garage remote.

Wow. She peered up at the stately brick Tudor. "All those gables and arches. This is a perfect house for twinkle lights, although not as easy to light as my family's house."

"True." He leaned forward to study it, too. "Maybe we should start with the easiest part."

"Which would be?"

"The garage."

Okay, she really shouldn't be so intrigued by

him. "Good idea. How about I do the garage? That will leave you to do the gables of the second story."

"Deal." He motored into the garage, out of the gently falling snow and shut off the engine. He unclicked his belt, drawing her attention to his strong, perfectly shaped hands. Healing hands.

He's a doctor, she reminded herself as she opened her door and hopped down, remembering one of the first items on her dream man list. Not a doctor. Mostly because Nick had been studying to be a doctor, too, but that didn't change the fact. Michael was a doctor. Right there, that should put him on her no way list.

It was ridiculous, because he was on her no way list. Intellectually she knew that, but tell that to her heart. The shivery feeling returned as he brushed close, watching her help Macie down from the backseat. She felt his presence like the other half of her soul.

"Let's go in and warm up." The low notes of his voice had become familiar, the sound she most wanted to hear. His hand settled into the small of her back, lightly guiding her as if he did it every day. He unlocked the door. "We need to formulate a decorating plan."

"A plan sounds good." There she was, being lame again. His nearness made her dizzy. She forced her feet forward and followed a skipping

Macie into the house. The beep, beep of a security system barely penetrated her foggy brain as she slipped out of her coat. Macie took it from her and disappeared deeper into the house. Michael punched in a code, it silenced and she tumbled into the kitchen.

Amazing. Long black-and-gold marble counters, gleaming stainless appliances, pendant lights hanging like icicles over the island. Ropes of red Christmas lights marched along hand-carved cherrywood cabinets and led the way to the family room where a festive tree came to life when Macie knelt down to flip the switch. Twinklers flashed in a slow cadence, shining on glass ornaments. A delicate angel topped the tree, holding a hymnbook, mouth open as if in song.

"See?" Macie gestured with her casted arm to beneath the tree. "I put a blanket there for when my kitten comes so she'll have a soft place to sleep on Christmas morning."

"That's a very good idea." Her boots squeaked on the polished hardwood. It took all her willpower to keep her heart still when she slipped by Michael.

"On Christmas Eve before I go to bed," Macie chattered on, kneeling before the tree, "I'm gonna put out a bowl of milk so my kitten won't get hungry. She'll have to wait for me all the way until morning."

"That's thoughtful, Macie." She couldn't help brushing a light brown shock of hair from the girl's face. Gentle affection for the child filled her up, brimming over. "You are going to make a great pet owner. That's a very important thing to be."

"I know," Macie said in her singsong voice, beaming with hope brighter than the Christmas tree. "Do you know what? First, I'm gonna hold her and hug her. Then we're gonna open the rest of my presents together. I'm gonna love her and love her."

"Sounds like a perfect plan." The sweet little black and the darling little calico were getting more than a home. They were getting a great child to love. "Do you have a name picked out?"

"Um, I can't decide." Macie scrunched up her face, thinking hard, as she smoothed the blanket lovingly. "First I thought Princess, but that's when I wanted a white kitty. I just might wanna name a striped kitty Tigger, but I need to think up more striped names."

"There's Bee, as in honeybee. And Jailbird." Chelsea did her best to focus on the job at hand, kneeling down beside the girl. But her ears picked up the muffled pad of Michael's footsteps in the kitchen, she heard the microwave humming and the tap of phone keys as he texted someone.

"Not Jailbird." Macie laughed.

"Let's see. What else is striped? Candy canes."

Her voice sounded tinny and distant to her ears. The strengthened awareness between her and Michael came to the forefront, blocking out all else. Her senses fine-tuned to catch his every movement, his every breath. "You could always go with a nonstriped name. Duchess. Clementine. Leopold."

"Leopold? That's a boy's name!" With a giggle, the girl bounced to her feet, shining in the jeweled lights of the tree. "Maybe Christmas. Kitty Whiskers. Jingle Bell."

"Brilliant. I like the holiday theme." She felt the tractor-beam tug of Michael's gaze. He stood with phone in his hand, a kettle on the stovetop rumbling behind him, three mugs lined up on the counter in front of him.

He's the one, her heart whispered. *The one and only.* She wasn't ready for this, she was panicking big-time, but she couldn't stop the quiet and abiding love filling her up like Christmas wishes, like dreams meant to come true.

"I think Hey You has a nice ring to it." He swept the kettle off the stove and filled two of the cups. The scent of mint tea rose with the steam. "What? Why isn't that a good name?"

"Oh, Daddy." Macie shook her head at him, feigning disapproval. "Is that hot chocolate for me?"

"Yes, I'm putting you on marshmallow duty."

He tore open a cocoa packet and dumped it into the third mug.

"Do we have the puffy ones or the colored ones?" She opened what looked like a pantry door. Yep—full of boxes and cans and two bags of marshmallows.

"I don't know what your grammy got when she went shopping for us." He poured water, set down the kettle and stirred. Riveting, seeing Michael in the kitchen moving with the ease of a man used to being in the kitchen. It was easy to picture him whipping up a meal. Too bad seeing his domestic side made him even more attractive. She couldn't help falling in love with him a little more.

"Ooh! The little colored ones." Happy, Macie padded over to her father, clutching the bag. She tried to open it, but it was awkward with her cast, so he did it for her and handed her the bag. Up on tiptoes she went, shaking colorful miniature puffs into the steaming chocolate. When one fell on the counter, she popped it into her mouth. Cute.

"What are you trying to do? Make a marshmallow mountain?" Michael arched an eyebrow as he circled around the marble island. "Leave some for next time. That's going to spoil your dinner."

"Do kittens like marshmallows?" Macie asked, crinkling up the bag.

"Probably not good for them," Chelsea answered, her breath squeaking out of her as Michael drew near. Her fingers curled around the handle of the cup he held out for her. Peppermint scented the air. What had she been saying? She couldn't remember because she couldn't think. Likely it was impossible to think with so much panic charging through her system.

"Here, this will help you warm up. Sorry, mint is the only kind I have."

"It's the kind I like best, too." She really needed to ignore all the things they had in common and focus on the differences. On all the reasons why she shouldn't be feeling what she felt for him. "I couldn't help noticing you received a text."

"A few actually. One was from Kelsey's mother." He took a sip of tea, watching her over the rim. "She said you texted her this morning, just to check on her, as a friend."

"She's nice. Anyone would do the same." Her expressive eyes crinkled slightly in the corners, betraying her concern. "I didn't think. Maybe it's not appropriate."

"You were checking on her mom, and it was kind of you." He swallowed hard, against emotions that threatened to run him over like a wild herd of stampeding reindeer. "If she texted you, then you know little Kelsey's prognosis is grim."

"Her mom told me." Compassion made her impossibly more beautiful. How could his heart resist falling completely?

"Kelsey's holding her own today. That's good news." He took a sip of hot tea, hoping the fresh mint taste rolling across his tongue would divert his attention. It failed. Miserably. "When all else fails, pray."

"That's what I've been doing."

"Me, too." As hard as he knew how. "Tomorrow we should get the rest of the lab work back. Then I'll have a better idea of how much time she has."

"What a hard thing to have to face. Her parents—" Chelsea fell silent, pain filling her gentle blue eyes. "You must want to do everything you can to keep her here on this earth."

"True." His gaze followed Macie, who carried her cup piled high with melting marshmallows to the tree. She sat down, cross-legged, staring at the blanket where she hoped her Christmas kitty would lay, dreaming of her new best friend—friends, but she didn't know that yet. "There is no greater blessing."

"Agreed." Chelsea sipped her cup, watching Macie poke her finger into the marshmallow fluff and stir it around.

The doorbell chimed, right on time. He set the mug on the edge of the breakfast bar. "Be right back."

"Is it Grammy?" Macie looked up, licking the fluff off her finger.

"Probably not." He wove through the house and

opened the door. Pete Dubronsky stood on the threshold and held out a key.

"Found this in a magnetic box on the car frame," the mechanic explained. "The poor old car just needed a new battery and it's good to go, for now. But those spark plugs are gonna have to be replaced before long."

"I'll tell her. Thanks, Pete. Bye." He took the key, aware of the whisper of her presence behind him. The snowy walkway, the mechanic stomping away, the icy wind on his face felt distant as Chelsea shouldered in, mouth agape, surprise drawing adorable crinkles into her lovely face.

"What did you do?" She reached for her coat on the wooden tree. "You had my car fixed."

"You heard him. It was just a battery." He didn't want her to read too much into it, or else how could he keep his heart guarded? "Pete owed me a favor. His oldest son used to be a patient."

"Used to be?"

"Four years cancer-free." That felt good to say, good to remember that stories could end happily. Happy endings were what he worked so hard for, prayed so hard for. Standing next to her made it easier to see that. "So I called Pete and he was happy to help. Now you owe me."

"I guess I do." Thoughtful, she studied the car parked in the driveway. Hard to guess what she was thinking. Had he tipped his hand? Revealed too much? She bent her head to work her coat zipper. "This can only mean one thing. I'd best get working on the lights so I can even the score."

"Now you're talking." A painful twist in the vicinity of his heart tore through him, weakening his knees. He reached behind her, close enough to feel the silk of her hair against his cheek, and snagged his coat from the tree. "I'll open up the garage, haul out the ladders. You and Macie can get the lights."

"Deal." She pulled a red knit cap out of her pocket and tugged it on. "Macie can be my light stringing partner, right, Mace?"

"Right." The sprite joined them, going up on tiptoes to fetch her coat.

"Guess I know where I stand." He buttoned up. "You could have picked me."

"Tempting, but I had to go with my heart." She splayed her hand gently over the top of Macie's soft head.

"Clearly I can't compete."

"Not even close," Chelsea assured him with a wink. "But you are second-best."

"Considering the company, that's a compliment." He gave his daughter's hat a small tug, unable to douse his affection for his daughter or for the woman. He grabbed the extra garage remote from the doorside table and closed the door, following the females out into gently falling snow.

Chelsea. He wanted to picture her in his life. To imagine a future with her in this house, laughing with Macie, sipping tea in his kitchen. To think what his days could be like with her in them.

"Look, Chelsea," Macie called, holding her arms straight out, turning in circles on the driveway. "I'm twirling."

"Oh, I love to twirl, too!" Chelsea lifted her arms gracefully and spun, a flash of navy coat, light chestnut hair and red mittens. Her laughter joined Macie's. "I forgot how fun this is, but I'm getting dizzy."

"Me, too." Macie hadn't sounded this happy in years.

Don't even think about the reason why, he told himself, opening the garage door. He wasn't looking for another relationship, he feared he would just mess it up, so why was Chelsea still here? He didn't need help with the lights, what he needed was harder to define. He couldn't let her go, not yet, so he hauled out his ladder and the extra one Dad had left for him. No need to tell Chelsea that his father had planned to help him with the lights. He found both females on their backs on the snowy front lawn.

"Or maybe Happy Face." Macie swished her arms, making angel's wings.

"I like pet names that are people names," Chelsea said thoughtfully as she moved her feet, making an angel's gown. "I named my first kitty Pearl. I was a little younger than you when my mom and dad took us to pick out Christmas kittens. Sara Beth and I each got to choose one kitten. She named hers Hank."

"Hmm." Macie carefully climbed out of the snow angel she'd made, leaving a handprint in the middle. She bent over to swipe it away. "Pearl. I like it."

"Excellent." Chelsea rose, leaving a perfect angel impression behind. "Michael, looks like you're ready for us. Although I'm not sure anyone could be, since Macie and me are an awesome combination."

"Hey, I'm blown away," he agreed, since it was the truth. Blown away. Captivated. Wishing for what could never be. He mustered every ounce of strength he had to hide the truth, lock it up in his heart and throw away the key. He leaned the ladder against the garage wall and gave it a shake, checking that it was secure. "Why don't you bring your awesomeness over here? The lights aren't gonna hang themselves."

"Stand back. Our awesomeness really is a powerful force." Chelsea sauntered over with laughing eyes and the glow of happiness leaving a lovely pink blush on her heart-shaped face. "C'mon, Macie. You can be the supervisor. Let's get these lights up."

He held out his hand to help her get started on the ladder. The instant her smaller palm rested on his, the shock to his heart was nothing compared to the recognition in his soul. Wow, he thought, as she let go and rose up the rungs. Snow dotted her red cap and clung to her hair. Framed by the swirling, falling flakes, she was the steady, incomparable center his whole world turned around.

He didn't want to feel this way. Not one bit. The weight of the past clung to him as he marched into the shelter of the garage. Good, a little distance was what he needed. Time to get some air, try to clear his head and figure out a way to get a handle on this. He ripped off the top of a plastic storage bin and pulled out a tangle of icicle lights.

But what he felt had become too incredible to ignore. He had a bad track record with relationships, and yet he'd never wanted anything as much. He shook out the lights, found the end and handed it up to her.

"Hey, you're pretty handy." Nothing was more dear than her smile. She plucked the lights from him and got to work. "Maybe you have awesomeness, too."

No, the awesomeness was purely hers. He fetched the second ladder, climbed up and helped her string dangling icicles in accordance with Macie's helpful directions.

* * *

"No, Daddy!" Macie bent down to scoop a mitten full of snow and tossed it up in the air to rain over her. Too cute. Chelsea looked up from the far end of the front porch, a string of lights in hand. Once the fistful of snow had stopped falling over her head, she dashed down the walkway. "Not over the rail, *over* the rail."

"Is it me? I'm missing something." His buttery voice resonated with humor.

When his gaze fastened on hers, wham. The earth shook beneath her feet. Judging by his lack of reaction, she was apparently the only one who felt it. "She means over, as in wrap around."

Understanding dawned on his gorgeous face. "Got it. Is this better?"

"Yup." Macie collapsed onto the bottom porch step and propped her chin up with the heels of her hands. "I'm hungry."

"And it's getting dark." Chelsea began winding her string of lights around the porch banister, mirroring Michael's movements at the other end. "I can't believe the whole day has whizzed by."

"Time flies when you're having fun," Michael said, bent over his work. "Why don't you stay and eat with us?"

"Uh—" Yes, she wanted to stay. What was wrong with her that she didn't want to leave?

"No need to panic, I'm not cooking." He reached

the middle of the porch banister, at the end of his light string. "Mom brought over a casserole yesterday. We'll warm it up. It's pretty tasty."

"And so's dessert," Macie added, clasping her hands together. "Please, you gotta stay."

"I'd love to." Had she really used the word *love?* Yikes. Not at all what she meant. "But I have chores waiting at home. Stuff to pick up at the grocery store. Sisters who can't get by without me. That kind of thing."

"Right." He looked as if he didn't believe her a bit. He stood there, towering in the dark like everything a woman could ever want—except for one thing. He wasn't watching her with affection warm in his eyes. Just friendship. He shrugged. "That's too bad. Maybe another time."

"Sure. Right." The wonder of the afternoon clung to her, even as the wind grew colder, pummeling her as she made one final wind of the lights, took a step and plugged them into the waiting prong. "We're done."

"With the first story, anyway." Michael's hand settled on her shoulder, his touch a brief squeeze imparting friendship, when she wanted it to be more.

So much more. What's wrong with me? she asked herself as his boots tapped across the porch. I'm independent, I have a no-man plan, I have different goals. Why am I feeling like this?

She didn't know what had happened to her heart. Men had a way of getting in the way of a woman's goals. She didn't know why she wanted him to love her. She could only pray he was starting to feel the same way. She clapped her gloved hands together to warm them, watching Michael plug the industrial power cord into the end of the light string.

"Are you awesome ladies ready?" he asked, unaware of her interest. Unaware of how the afternoon had changed things between them—on her end, anyway. Being near him rocked her like an emotional wave. A wave that threatened to carry her away when she wanted to stay firmly rooted to the ground. She turned to Macie and held out her hand. "C'mon, cutie."

"Okay!" The girl bounded to her feet, slipped her mittened fingers around Chelsea's and together they hurried down the driveway to get the full effect.

"Ready?" Michael called from the twilight porch.

"Now, Daddy!" Macie shouted.

Lights flashed on, and Chelsea blinked at the sight. Pure white glowing icicles rimmed the entire first story from the garage to the far corner of the house, bringing brightness where there was once shadow. Michael stood in the middle of it, and yet she felt alone in the dark.

Chapter Fourteen

This day had been a huge mistake. Massive. Gargantuan. Chelsea felt Macie's fingers slip from hers as the girl scuffled down the snowy driveway to meet her father.

"It's exactly right." Macie sighed happily. "Now it's just like Christmas."

"It really is." Michael became a tall silhouette against the background twinkling lights as the last dregs of twilight slipped away.

It was better that she could hardly see him. Really, much better. Chelsea dug into her pocket for her keys, needing to look away, needing to be busy as he stalked toward her. She prayed the darkness could hide her feelings as his footsteps squeaked closer on the snow and she tried her other pocket. Nothing. Where were her keys?

"Looking for this?" He towered over her, blotting out the sky. Something metallic glinted faintly in the ambient light.

"Right. Yes." She snatched her spare key from his gloved fingertips, keeping her head down, feeling vulnerable to him and wishing with all her might that she didn't. The last time she'd felt like this had been disastrous. Nick hadn't been part of her plans, either. Now, what else was she missing? *Think, Chelsea.* "Oh, my bag."

Apparently, she was about to lose her mental faculties right along with her heart.

"I'll get it!" Macie danced through the reflection of the lights on the walkway and disappeared onto the shadowed porch.

"It's been a good afternoon." Michael spoke into the pause between them before it could become an uncomfortable silence. "It didn't hurt that you spent it with us."

"Well, it was fun hanging out with Macie." The quip was all she could think of to hide her feelings.

"Just Macie, huh?" His soft chuckle warmed the chill from the evening air. "Not me?"

"Really, do I have to answer that?" She leaned against the icy side of her car, amusement hiding something shadowed in her eyes. "I still have to see you in the clinic twice a week."

"And there's the food drive." Something more than friendship lit his gaze, his caring gaze which searched her face.

Okay, she was imagining that, right?

"I'm harder to avoid than you think." There it was again in the melted chocolate tone.

"Too bad." The quip died on her tongue. No, maybe she had it wrong, she thought as he moved in to brush a lock of hair from her eyes. His nearness sent shivers of sweetness through her. His touch was the most tender thing she'd known.

"I've got to swing by the grocery store on the way home, so I really have to go." Distance was the best move. Stumble back into the car, plop onto the seat, keep a friendly smile on her face and drive away fast. "Sara Beth needs milk for dinner."

Great, Chelsea, now you're babbling, she thought, fumbling with her key.

"Be safe." He moved in, one gloved hand on the door. "See you tomorrow in the office. Please pray for Kelsey tonight."

"She's on my prayer list." She wanted to sound breezy, unaffected, the kind of woman who never handed over her heart to a man.

"Thanks." He closed her door and not even the steel barrier of the car could snap the connection she felt to him.

"Bye!" Macie fluttered her fingers, the glittery stickers on her cast catching the glow from the icicle lights. "Bye, Princess Chelsea."

"Bye, Princess Macie," she called through the window glass, started her car, which rolled over on the first try and jetted out of the driveway. She glanced in her rearview mirror at the brick Tudor half swathed in white lights and the man standing in the driveway, watching her go. The man she could love, if she let herself.

"There you are!" Sara Beth looked up from the stove the instant Chelsea tumbled in through the garage door. "I was just about to text you and remind you dinner is almost ready."

"It smells divine." Chelsea shrugged out of her coat, grateful to be home. Doubly grateful for her sister's gentle smile. Everything was better when she was with her sisters. She plopped the single grocery sack on the counter. "Here's the milk. Is that Mom's chicken and dumplings?"

"Johanna's favorite. I thought she needed cheering up." Sara Beth stirred something in a pot, set down the ladle and plunked on the glass cover. "She's been a little down this afternoon. Nothing serious and no idea what's up, and believe me, I tried to get it out of her, but I couldn't resist the urge to cheer her up with food."

"Excellent. Can't think of a better cure." Chelsea plopped her bag on the breakfast bar. "Where's Meg? I'm on barn chore duty with her."

"She's out doing your share of the work, but that's okay. Dad offered to help her." Sara Beth tugged open the oven door and peered inside. A stronger aroma of seasoned chicken, creamy gravy and doughy dumplings sailed into the air.

Yum. Chelsea's stomach growled harder. Maybe good food and her family's company would take her mind off Michael—or more accurately, what she'd glimpsed in his eyes.

"Did you get all your shopping done?" Sara Beth closed the oven door.

"No, not even close." The wonderful afternoon rolled back in perfectly clarity. Michael's kindness, the heated iron pressure of his arm tucked against hers in the sleigh, the icy wind burning her face, the love taking root in her heart. Was she ready to share those things with anyone, even her sisters? Could she admit to being so foolish? She opened her mouth, but the words didn't come out. They stayed stuck like peanut butter on her tongue.

"Go see what we did in the living room." Sara Beth wandered over to the cabinets and began counting out enough plates for the table. "Johanna got the brilliant idea of putting out Mom's ceramic Christmas towns, you know, the light up ones? Johanna's up in the attic digging out a few more pieces."

"If you don't need help here, I'll go lend a hand."

"Go on. I've got this." Sara Beth dealt plates around the kitchen table like a pro. She sidestepped dear old Bayley, who'd fallen sleep next to Dad's chair. "Maybe Johanna will open up to you."

It was hard to think of her youngest sister hurting. She knew just how Johanna felt the moment she stepped into the living room. The brilliant Christmas tree glowed with rich color, presents beneath the lowest branches gleamed faintly from the twinkle lights and half of a ceramic village sat on the mantel. Mom could have been here; it felt as if she'd just walked out of the room.

Burt purred a greeting as she walked by the couch. She stopped to scrub his ears on her way out of the room. She followed the faint scuffling sounds until she found Johanna in the attic behind a pile of cardboard boxes coated with dust.

"I can't find them." Johanna blinked hard and fast and turned her back, poking through another box. "They have to be here, right?"

"Right." Chelsea picked her away across the bare floor, around an old chest and the pile of cardboard boxes. "Tell me where to start and I'll help you look."

"Good. Check out any dusty box. I definitely could use the help." Johanna gave a surreptitious sniffle, pawing through the box in front of her. "Remember how Mom would put her towns up every year?"

"Are you kidding? She had them everywhere." Chelsea opened the first container she saw and ignored the puff of dust when she pried off the lid. "Dad used to tease her that if she kept collecting pieces, there wouldn't be any space left for us in the living room."

"I know. She had so many pieces. Why am I not finding them?" Johanna's attempt at lightness failed. "I just want Christmas like it used to be."

"It's impossible, sister dear." She pawed through the container and pulled out an art project. Not what she was looking for, but the little ceramic hand from decades ago made her gasp. "Look. Mom saved this."

"Did you find them?" Johanna dropped what she was doing and swerved around the pile of boxes. Hope sparkled in her eyes bright with unshed tears, tears she blinked away with great determination. "Oh, I'm so relieved. Is it the church with the stained glass steeple? I—" She skidded to a stop.

"It's yours." Chelsea brought the piece of plaster into the fall of light from the overhead bulb. "These are your little handprints."

"I made that in kindergarten." Johanna sidled in, silken dark hair falling like a curtain to shield her face. "For Mother's Day."

"Let's see what it says." The letters written in the plaque were hard to read. Chelsea shifted the prints until the words came clear beneath the overhead light. "It says, 'I love you, Mommy.'"

"I remember telling that to my teacher when she asked what to write for me." Johanna swiped at her eyes, her battle lost to hold back her grief. "What's this on the back?"

Chelsea flipped it over to see a sticky note clinging to the backside. In Mom's writing, she read, "'For the scrapbook. Write down the memory of Johanna giving this to me after Grant and the girls made a Mother's Day breakfast. Big blue eyes, so sincere she said, God gave me the best mommy.'"

"He really did." Tears rolled down Johanna's cheeks, beautiful tears of love. "Look, this container is full of Mom's things. How did this get up here anyway?"

"Remember Aunt Gretchen packed up Mom things for Dad?" Just after the funeral. "It was too painful for any of us, so she did it and brought the things up here."

"Here's a ribbon from one of Sara Beth's first riding competitions." Johanna knelt before the bin, gently moving things aside. "Look at this."

"A picture of us." Chelsea had to swipe her eyes to see the photograph clearly, a picture of a happy young family in matching holiday sweaters. "It was from that Christmas when we got the kittens. You were a baby."

"I was so cute, even if I do say so myself. Look at that happy face." Johanna leaned in to marvel at the faces, captured in smiles, frozen in time when Mom was young and beautiful. "This is the way I always remember her. With her hair in soft curls, her wide smile like Julia Roberts's, her joy just beaming out of her."

"Look at Meg as a toddler." She held the old picture with care, studying the two-year-old with big doe eyes standing alongside the little six-year-old she herself had been.

"Oh, look at Sara Beth and her thick beautiful hair. Adorable." Johanna caught a tear before it could fall. "Do you ever wish you could go back and do things differently?"

"All the time." Like not fall in love with Michael. Like not leave Mom before her final illness. Yes, life do-overs would be merciful.

"I shouldn't have gone back to vet school after that last Christmas." Johanna's lovely face crinkled with misery. "I should have put my last semester on hold and stayed here with her."

"You were in the last year of vet school." Chelsea laid the picture carefully down on a box top. "If you hadn't finished, it would have put you so far behind."

"I should have been here with her."

"I know how you feel." Why hadn't she seen this earlier? Maybe because Johanna was hiding her guilt the same way Chelsea was, trying to move forward but it was like an anchor holding her back. "I was in the middle of my residency. I feel the same way."

"I can't let it go, Chelsea. I just wish I'd known."

She saw herself in Johanna, and really felt what Sara Beth had told her. "Neither of us knew. Remember, her oncologist said she had maybe a year to eighteen months to live after her last round of chemo. That's what we all thought. Even believing she had all that time, I was torn, needing to continue my schooling and wanting to be home with Mom."

"Exactly." Johanna lowered her hands, revealing her tearstained face. "Mom used to say to me, 'Chelsea's sticking with her program. You stick with yours.' I did, I was counting down the months until I could be home and help her, but then Sara Beth called saying Mom had that infection. If I'd known, I would have stayed with her. I would have—" A tear dripped off her chin. Her shoulders slumped with the weight of her regret. A regret Chelsea shared.

"But the thing is, we couldn't have known. Only God knows the future. We all thought we had more time. We did the best we could." A weight felt lifted off her shoulders. She wrapped her arm around Johanna, drawing her close.

"We were blessed to have her for a mom." Johanna sighed as she gestured toward the photograph.

"Very blessed," Chelsea agreed. "I wouldn't trade her for anything."

"Me, either. Thanks, Chels, I feel better."

"Me, too."

"Hey, I've figured out a gift for Dad." Johanna's chin wobbled.

They studied the photograph together. Dad, so happy, Mom so vibrant. Little girls, safe and sheltered and loved. Yes, Chelsea thought, it would be a perfect gift. "This was our first Christmas all together as a family."

"Not that I remember it."

"It was good. Christmas kittens. The squeal of three little girls when we woke up Christmas morning to see the huge pile of presents under the tree." Chelsea didn't know if she was laughing or crying. Maybe both. "You were blinking in Mom's arms, trying to wake up and see what was going on, while Dad handed out presents."

"Those times are never really gone, are they?" Johanna's smile wobbled along with her chin.

"No, I guess not. They are still here within us." Proof true love never died. It was up to them to carry their love for their mother into the future. "If we find a photographer to blow up this pic, we could get a cool frame."

"And hang it over the living room fireplace," Johanna finished. "C'mon, let's go tell Sara Beth. I think she'll love it."

"You go ahead." Chelsea handed Johanna the picture. "I'll finish up here finding the rest of the town pieces."

"Thanks, Chels." Johanna clutched the photograph carefully, a great treasure, proof of love gone by and love everlasting.

Chelsea swiped the dampness from her eyes, listening to her sister's footsteps pound away. The attic didn't feel as empty or lonely as she pulled a ceramic church from its nest of tissue paper. Maybe heaven really was closer than you thought. Maybe it was always close to your heart.

The living room felt snug this time of night with a low fire dying in the grate, Bayley lightly snoring on his bed by the hearth and the rest of her family nearby, watching television. The drone of a legal drama murmured in the background as she finished her email to Susan and hit Send. A lot of local businesses had pledged funds for the town food bank. She and Susan planned on doing a pickup during their lunch hour tomorrow.

"Hey, Burt." She reached over to the cat on the

couch beside her. His eyes glowed in the light of her tablet computer. "Thanks for hanging out with me tonight, big guy."

Burt purred rustily in answer, closing his eyes when she hit his favorite spot behind his right ear.

Bing, went her iPad, signaling a new email. "It's probably from Susan."

Burt kept on purring as she checked her screen. She blinked at the name sitting at the top of her inbox. Michael Kramer. Her fingers moved of their own accord, opening the message.

Thought you might like to see the finished product. His words marched across her screen. My dad saw me struggling with the gables and stopped to help. I think it looks pretty good.

She clicked on the attachment and a picture popped onto her screen. His house rimmed in lights looked like a Christmas card, merry and bright.

The best part is the garage, if I say so myself. She typed and hit Send, realizing she was smiling. Realizing she missed him like a physical pain.

"Hey, you're not still working, are you?" Sara Beth waltzed around the corner, her dark hair shining in the firelight. "You have your iPad out. You are working. I know you're not watching a movie on it."

"I was working, now I'm emailing." She had the sudden urge to close the picture so her sister wouldn't see or guess the truth, but she was too late as that wily Sara Beth snatched the tablet from her.

"Wow, I thought you weren't interested in Michael."

"I'm sure it's a passing thing. Here today, gone tomorrow." She held out her hand, wanting her iPad back. "You know men and love. You're smart not to count on them."

"Sometimes." Sara Beth eased onto the cushion beside Burt, handed back the iPad and scratched the cat's head. "There are men who are dependable. Men who stick with their wives when they're sick. Men who try their best to raise their children."

"I know." She did. She took one last glance at Michael's house and the afternoon flooded back. The warm, comforting feeling when he took her hand to help her into the sleigh, of his iron warmth as she snuggled against his side and how right it had felt, like coming home. And especially dangerous was remembering the moments when they laughed together. Things with him came easily and had gone way too fast. "Whatever this is, I have to nip it in the bud."

"Before you get hurt?"

"Before I fall in love with him," she corrected. Sara Beth's understanding meant everything. "It hasn't happened yet."

"So, what are you going to do? Retreat from him and throw yourself into your work, or just shoot him down kindly? Do you really think that will work?"

"Yes, and it's the sensible thing." The safe thing. She turned off her tablet and set it on the coffee table. "I've always been able to stop myself from feeling this way. This is the first time—" She bit her lip, not wanting to bring up the past.

"The first time since Nick?" Sara Beth asked gently.

Unable to speak, Chelsea nodded. She could still hear Nick's angry words before he slammed her apartment door and walked out of her life. *Do you know how hard it was to love you, Chelsea? You and your plans and your lists. God knows I've tried, but you're not worth it.* That's what three years of love and trusting Nick had come to in the end. That's where setting aside her plans had led her.

She blew out a shivery breath. Even now, his words still hurt. She knew when he said them, he was angry and hurting too, but that didn't excuse him. She'd risked her life's dreams for him only to have them come crashing down. He hadn't loved her enough. What were the chances another man couldn't either? She thought of her carefully designed future in a document on her iPad. Finish med school. Check. Finish residency. Check. Help sick kids, which was her life now. That was a fine plan, one she'd designed long ago to keep her safe.

"What if I put my heart into someone and love them with all I am, and it doesn't work out?" she asked her sister. "I'm afraid to take the risk. Every time I have the chance at love, I stop it, right here. I nip it in the bud. But with Michael—"

"He's different."

"Yes." Nothing she'd ever felt had been like this. "I want to, but I don't think I can take the risk."

"Take the risk, Chelsea?"

"It's the smartest thing. It's always worked before." She thought of her parent's marriage, the way they had been utterly devoted to one another. "I want what Mom and Dad had. True love, happily-ever-after, two hearts, one soul."

"I know. That's what I want, too." Sara Beth lifted Burt into her lap and scooted closer. "But if you don't take the risk, then you'll never have a chance of getting it. The only thing you'll have is your well-planned life. Is that what you want?"

"Hey, there's nothing wrong with a well-planned life."

"Right, but there's only one problem with it," Sara Beth said as Burt purred loudly. "God is the one who plans your life, not you."

"Okay, but I live by the proverb, *A man's heart plans his way, but the Lord directs his steps.*"

"There are many plans in a man's heart, nevertheless the Lord's counsel will stand."

They smiled together in the glow of the Christmas tree. If only she could forget Michael's kindness and caring. Even now her soul fluttered, wishing for what could be.

He's not the one, she told her heart and prayed it would listen.

Chapter Fifteen

Monday morning surrounded her in blinding brightness. Sun glanced off snow on the clinic roof and winked off the thin sheet of ice layering the parking lot. Chelsea rolled into the back parking lot, spotted the six other employee vehicles parked in the sunshine and blew out a breath of frustration. Michael's SUV was not one of them. He wasn't here, which meant he wasn't safely tucked behind his closed office door where he usually was this time of day. Which meant he could be anywhere, even turning into the alley this very minute, which meant she was vulnerable to bumping into him.

So much for all her careful planning. She rolled to a stop next to Susan's SUV while the radio belted out the weather report. "We're in the path of the jet stream, folks, so batten down the hatches. We're in for a big blow by the end of the week. I'm dreaming of a white Christmas."

She turned off the engine, the radio silenced and she unclicked her belt. What were the chances she could get into the building, to her office and close the door for some preclinic hours organizing before Michael pulled in? Maybe he wasn't even coming to the office this morning, with Kelsey ill in the hospital. Kelsey. That reminded her.

Before she could forget, she yanked her tablet computer out of her bag, cast a furtive glance at the alley to make sure the coast was clear and flipped to her daily to-do list. She typed in, *call to check on Kate*. This was what she liked best about being a small-town pediatrician, the chance to get to know people and to help them when she could.

A chill crept into the car as she turned off her iPad. Now, if the coast was still clear—

A rap of knuckles on the window beside her made her jump. Michael stared in through the ice-glazed glass. "Hey, are you okay?"

"Fine, yeah." Flustered, she jammed her iPad into her bag and opened the door. He smelled great, like pine and snow. Why was that the first thing she noticed? It was good to see him. She'd missed him. Two signs she was in deeper than she realized.

She stared at her boots, at her hands, wait—she couldn't forget about the kitten stuff.

"Here, this is for you." She reached across the seat and tugged out the shrink-wrapped gift bundle. "I buzzed by the vet clinic on my way here and picked this up for you. All the handouts I told you about are in there."

"Wow, this is great." He took the bundle and closed the door for her with his elbow. "Thanks, Chelsea."

"It's the least I can do for the guy who had my car fixed." She locked the door, keeping her back firmly turned to him. No need to let him see how hard this was, knowing she loved him. And knowing if she looked at him she couldn't miss the gentle caring in his gaze. She gave the key a firm turn. "It's a starter pack. Kitten food, kitten treats, toys, two fleece cat blankets, two food dishes, which are pink so I thought Macie would like them, and a little litter box with a bag of starter litter. Everything you need."

"This looks like more than the average starter pack."

"Blame Meg and Johanna. It's their fault." Not that she wasn't responsible too, but she didn't want to add that.

"Tell them thanks from me." He adjusted his longer stride, keeping at her side. "Are you sure you're all right?"

Ignore the caring notes in his voice, she thought, steeling her spine. She could do this. She could try not to care so much for him. "I'm good, just got a lot on my mind. It's a busy week with work, ensemble practice and after—"

"—bagging grocery sacks for the needy in our congregation," he finished amiably, as if they didn't just breathe in synchrony, but thought alike. "I'm looking forward to that. I've always written a check for Steve and brought canned foods to service whenever it was asked, but it feels great to be a part of this."

"I can't argue." See? she thought. This wasn't terribly hard. As long as she kept her eyes on the ground and her heart closed up like a wrapped present before Christmas, she was good.

She stepped onto the curb. "Do you have all your shopping done?"

"Nearly, just a few things left to do. Hitting the pet store is one of them." He held the door for her.

"So the basket came just in time?"

"Something like that."

"The vet clinic's number is in the basket. You might want to put it in your cell. Johanna and Meg both said they'd be happy to answer any questions. The two of them love to give out advice." She sailed down the hallway. The agony was almost over now. She only had to hold it together a little bit longer. Keep it light and friendly. "Don't take this the wrong way, but you don't look like the kind of man who knows how to pick out a kitty condo."

"You'd be right about that. Do kitty condos come in pink?"

"No idea." *Don't laugh, don't look at him,* she thought firmly, fighting with everything she had. She hesitated by the break room door. Time to make her escape.

"Are you coming in?" Michael's hand landed on her shoulder. She could feel his gaze search her face as tangible as a touch.

"No, I've got a to-do list two miles long." It was nothing but the truth. "I'd better get started on it."

"Sure." His fingers gently squeezed, a show of encouragement. "I know how it is."

He really was a nice man, a good man. *Don't let that sway you, Chelsea.* She offered him a shrug, gave a little finger flutter and walked on wooden legs down the hallway. She couldn't feel her feet. She couldn't feel anything as she stumbled into her office. When she glanced back, he'd already disappeared inside the break room. She felt bereft without him, which was, well, ridiculous. Proof that her feelings were way out of proportion. Too much, too fast. That could only spell trouble.

Stick to your plan, Chelsea, she told herself, dropping into her chair. She turned on her desktop computer to check her schedule for the day. While it powered up, she spotted the corner of a manila envelope sticking out of her bag. She opened the flap and pulled out the old photograph of her family, the one she and Johanna had found in the attic.

"Here, thought you could use this." Michael strolled into her office, apparently she'd forgotten to close the door all the way. He set a cup on her desk. "I put in two sugars. I noticed that's the way you take it."

"Wow, thanks." She forgot not to look at him. He wore a white shirt, a deep red tie with Christmas trees on it and gray slacks.

He was the kind of man who wore a Christmas tie. She didn't know why that rocked her. Maybe she had better make a list of all the reasons he was wrong for her. Number one— Okay, she couldn't think of a reason but there had to be dozens of them.

"That's some picture." He leaned close. Too close. Maybe that was the reason she couldn't think. "You were cute."

"Is it me, or do you sound a little surprised?"

"I'm not. You look a lot like your mom."

Why did he have to say the one thing that would try and lasso her heart? "I think we all take after Mom. Sara Beth has her eyes, Johanna has her smile, Meg has her grace. We're going to get this blown up and framed for Dad's Christmas present. I'm taking it to the photo shop today and I'll beg them to get it done in time."

"I hope they can. He'll love it." Michael leaned

back on his heels, the cup in his hand steaming. His phone chimed and he bowed his head to read the screen, his sandy hair falling in a shock over his forehead. "Guess that's the starting bell on my workday. I'm expecting the rest of Kelsey's lab results. I'd better take care of this."

"Right. Thanks for the coffee."

"No problem." He strode down the hall, whistling "Jingle Bells."

"Dr. Mike!" Howie Lansing grinned from his wheelchair tucked in the corner of his hospital room. "I'm goin' home."

"Yes, you are." Michael stepped through the doorway. "You're doing great, kid. We don't want you around here anymore."

"I don't wanna be here!" The boy grinned wide, fidgeting with eagerness. "Do you know what's the first thing I'm gonnna do? Pet my dog."

"What's the second thing you're gonna do?"

"Mom's gonna make pizza for lunch and I'm gonna eat it."

"Sounds like an excellent plan to me. What about you, Nora?"

"First off, I'm going to pray to God in gratitude." Nora's happy smile said it all. She gave the duffle she was packing a zip, her work done. "Then I'm going to make pepperoni pizza."

"Important stuff. We'd better get you out of

here, fast." No orderly was around, so he seized the handles of Howie's wheelchair. "Let's get you home, kid."

"Okay." Howie started whistling "Jingle Bells" quite badly, but he wasn't the only one whistling.

I'm whistling "Jingle Bells," Michael realized, a little surprised.

"I can get that, Dr. Kramer." One of the orderlies rushed to take over.

"Thanks, Leo." Michael ruffled Howie's hair. "You have a merry Christmas. When I see you back for your checkup, you bring lots of pictures. I want to see what you got under the tree, okay?"

"Okay, and pictures of my dog, too." Howie waved as the orderly pushed him down the hall toward the elevator bank.

"Thank you." Nora squeezed his hand. "There aren't enough words."

"Just take care of him. No matter what, you call if you have even one question." Michael meant it. Howie was cancer-free, his prognosis was excellent. He planned to keep him that way.

Nora nodded, too choked up to speak further. She hurried down the hall, the elevator dinged and the doors opened. A tall man stepped out, knelt down and hugged Howie. Howie hugged his father back, Nora hugged her husband and the Lansing family headed off happy together.

His cell chimed, garnering his attention. He

waded down the busy corridor and read the text from his mom. Come for supper tonight. I'm making your favorite.

Ok, he tapped in, hit Send and walked into Kelsey's room. Her color looked better, she was munching on a fast-food taco and fries while hooked up to an IV.

"I hear someone will be able to go home for Christmas." He slipped his phone into his coat pocket. "I wonder who?"

"Me." Happiness lit her up. "Mom told me. It wasn't as bad as they thought. I prayed really hard."

"I did, too." He turned toward the family surrounding her. Mom, Dad and Grandma rose to their feet, abandoning their meals, concern marking their faces. "We need to rerun some tests, but it's nothing to worry about. I just need to confirm a few things."

"So it's still definite she'll be able to come home on Friday?" Kate gripped her hands until her knuckles turned white.

"That's the plan." He didn't want to say anything more because as good as the lab workers were, sometimes mix-ups happened. This was the kind of news he had to be sure of before he shared it. "You keep feeling better, Kelsey. You're doing an awesome job."

"It's cuz I pray." She bit into a fry, her bunny tucked in the crook of her arm.

He spent time answering parental concerns, reassuring them, and headed out, his rounds done. Nurses smiled at him as he strode by their station. Guess he was whistling again. It was easy to guess why, so he stopped.

He took the elevator to the first floor and wound his way to the small chapel, where candles danced and silence reigned. His movements echoed in the sanctuary as he settled onto one of the small pews. He'd spent so much time here, he couldn't count the number of children he'd prayed for. He went to bow his head to do so again, this time for Kelsey's sake, but the faint scent of strawberries and vanilla stopped him.

"Michael." Chelsea swept up the aisle, more striking than ever with her hair down and tumbling over her shoulders. She looked Christmassy in a green sweater and black slacks. Her boots whispered to a stop beside him. "I didn't know you were here."

"Just about to head back to the office." He had to fight the need to move closer to her. He stayed firmly on the cushioned bench. "The real question is what are you doing at the hospital?"

"It was a quiet morning, so Susan and I snuck out. We're rounding up the pledge checks from local businesses. Before she left, Steve's wife managed to wrangle a lot of money, which is great, so there's a lot of picking up to do." She shook her head. Maybe she was sounding a little too cheerful. She was trying too hard. "We stopped for lunch at the taco place two blocks away, I texted Kelsey's mom and brought them lunch."

"So that explained the tacos in the room."

"I remember what it was like when Mom was sick. So many of our friends and neighbors went out of their way to help. Just little things, but it made a huge difference. Guess this is my way of paying back. I help where I can." She fastened her gaze on the toes of her boots, just like she'd done this morning, avoiding him, putting distance between them.

Good idea. He truly cared for her. There was no way around it. "Sit down, we need to talk."

"Right. I can't argue with that. Maybe clearing the air is better than trying not to make eye contact." She set her bag on the floor and eased beside him. "You start."

"Sure, make me do the hard work," he quipped.

"Hey, it was your suggestion to talk, so you talk."

"Okay." He steeled his spine and prayed for the right words. This wasn't going to be easy, but it helped to know this was hard for her, too. "We had a good time together yesterday."

"We did." She stared fixedly at the pew back in front of her. "We get along so easily."

"Like breathing." He stared at the pew back, too. "Things between us feel like they have changed."

"Are you panicking, too?" She nearly whispered the words, and he understood. This wasn't easy for her. Once again, they were alike, the same in this.

That made it easier to open up. "A little panic, but mostly I'm not ready for this."

"Me, either." She whipped toward him, relief stark on her sweetheart's face. "I'm so relieved. Whew. I mean, you're great, Michael."

"You're greater." He liked that she smiled, that she sagged against the seat back, that he'd been able to erase the tension between them. They were both people of science. They could be logical about this. "I admit it. I really care for you, but I'm nowhere near ready for anything more than friendship."

"Exactly. I have my work, in case you haven't noticed I'm really focused on my work."

"You're preaching to the choir." They smiled together, two peas in a pod, more alike than he'd ever realized. "Relationships scare me."

"No kidding." No more hesitancy, no more distance, she pinned him with the dazzling force of her gaze. "I just finished my residency, I've got a lot to learn as a new doctor, and the school debt. That's a whole other consideration."

"Been there, done that." He rubbed a hand against the back of his neck. "After I lost Diana suddenly, one moment she was driving to get groceries, the next she'd slid on a patch of ice, I decided never to do a relationship again. I'd raise Macie on my own, practice medicine and that would be my life."

"The loss was too great?" she asked, the only one who could make him open up. Talking to her was as easy as breathing.

"Diana and I married young, and as time passed we grew into two very different people. People who wanted different things from life. She never understood my work, and I never want to feel as if I've disappointed anyone like that again."

"That had to be hard." Chelsea turned thoughtful. "Your work is serious and your patients need you. It takes commitment to do what you do, at least the way you do it."

"I want to do it the right way." He didn't have to explain it to her. "I guess we're alike that way."

"We are."

"I want to be honest with you." Concern dug deep in his chiseled features. "I don't ever want to hurt you, Chelsea."

"You aren't. Worrying about this was hurting me. I do care about you." She hoped the dip in her tone didn't betray exactly how close he'd become to her heart. "Yesterday was wonderful, but I just—"

"I know," he finished her sentence for her. "We don't want to ruin our working relationship."

"Exactly. We have to see each other all the time. There's no way around it between work and church and this is a small town. We could bump into each other at any time."

"All the same reasons I've been thinking." He reached out, giving her clear warning before his fingertips brushed a lock of hair out of her eyes. "I almost made a list."

"Me, too." She could have moved away—she should have moved away, but she sat riveted by his touch, slow, gentle, sweet. The most tender thing she'd ever known. "So I guess we've settled it. We're staying friends?"

"Friends." He folded the wayward strands behind her ear, and his gaze searched hers. In his kind blue eyes she saw what she feared most. He cared for her, he really did. Their agreement hadn't changed that. She still cared for him, too.

"Friends. This is just what we both want, so it's a good thing." She grabbed her bag, unable to explain the blinding pain cracking through her chest. Indigestion? Angina? Heartbreak? "Friends are always there for each other. Friends are always willing to lend a hand."

"Friends don't let you down." He stood when

she did, and for a moment she thought he had more to say, but he fell silent. She didn't say anything more either. This was the best solution. Sensible, logical, safe.

And sad, she thought as she stumbled into the aisle. "Susan's waiting. I'd better go."

"Right. See you later at the office, or at the food drive meeting?" He planted his hands on his hips, emphasizing the line of his shoulders, the strength of his broad chest, lost in the shadows. "I have prayers to say."

"Right. I'll say one for Kelsey. I'll say a dozen of them." How could she have forgotten? And why was she so rattled? Her boots carried her down the aisle that suddenly went blurry. She would pray in the car, but she needed distance to convince herself she'd made the right decision. When she reached the doorway, she risked a glance at the man nearly lost in shadow. Sorrow hit her like a punch as she hurried away.

Chapter Sixteen

The week before Christmas buzzed by in a whirl. Ensemble practice, last-minute Christmas gifts, begging the photography shop to have Dad's present ready by Christmas Eve. The only time Chelsea had run into Michael had been at the last food drive meeting where she and a dozen volunteers bagged and boxed canned goods for the needy in their church. Michael had been across the multi-purpose room and have given her a half smile in the bustle. That's all she'd seen of him all week.

Fine, so she really missed him, but this was a much better arrangement. Really. No worrying about things progressing too fast. No worrying about love letting her down. She squirted toothpaste on her purple toothbrush and ran it under the water. She was doing the smart thing. This was exactly how she wanted her life to go. Now all she had to do was convince her heart.

That might take time, but she could do it. She studied her reflection in the mirror—sleep-mussed hair, flannel pajamas and dark circles under her eyes. Okay, she hadn't been sleeping well. She had a lot on her mind, and it wasn't easy for a girl to convince herself not to follow her heart.

"Okay, I know when you're excited about something." Meg charged through the open door and yanked open a drawer and pawed through it. "Don't even think about denying it. Your denial won't work with me."

"Too bad. Denial is all I've got," she said around a mouthful of toothpaste. "Denial and nothing else. Sorry."

"Let's see. Maybe it's because it's Christmas Eve." Meg pawed around and came up with a hair elastic. "That's pretty exciting."

"Really, do we have to do this?" She worked her toothbrush around her back molars.

"We really do. Something has your eyes all lit up and I know it's not the food drive committee thing, because you finished it up early in the week." Meg gathered her bouncy hair into a ponytail and wound the elastic around it. "Let's see. What else could it be?"

"No idea." She spit into the sink, refusing to admit that Meg wasn't wrong.

"So, why else would you be smiling?" Meg leaned against the counter, sure of the answer.

"I'm not smiling, I'm brushing my teeth," Chelsea protested in vain.

"We got a check in the mail for Mom's scholarship," Meg grinned. "But I get the feeling that's not it either."

"Okay, you might as well say it." She waved her toothbrush in the air for emphasis. "You think it's because of Michael."

"I know it is. Sister dear, you've had a hangdog expression all week, and suddenly on Friday morning, his office day, you are lit up like a Christmas tree."

"I am not. Michael is a friend." It broke her heart to say the word, but it was for the best. "That's it."

"Sure." Meg rolled her eyes and opened the cabinet door. Footsteps padded in the hallway and she called out to the unseen sister around the corner. "Did you hear that, Johanna?"

"Yes, but I don't believe it. Not for a second." Johanna poked her head around the door frame, her dark hair caught in a sleek ponytail, fresh in from feeding the horses. "Chelsea, don't you know that you can't lead your heart, your heart leads you?"

"I totally agree with that," Meg chimed in.

"I'm taking the Fifth." Mostly because she wanted to disagree on principle, but time had not made her miss Michael any less. Distance from him had not stopped her affection for him. That just couldn't be good. She rinsed her toothbrush and plopped it into its holder.

"Hey, we have a problem. Have either of you two sleepyheads looked outside yet?" Johanna leaned against the door frame. "You know that storm they were predicting for tonight? Well, it came in *last* night. Surprise. Drifts are everywhere and it's still snowing. Sara Beth was going to check the news—"

"Grimes Road is closed," Sara Beth called up the stairwell. "We can't get to town. Johanna, I could use a hand down here."

"Coming." But Johanna didn't move from the door frame. "Well, if we can't get to town—"

"—then how do we get—" Meg interrupted.

"—Dad's gift?" Chelsea finished. "We can't."

"We can't drive out and no one could drive in." Johanna's forehead furrowed.

"Well, then we're stuck." Meg blew out a sigh.

"We don't even have the original picture to give him in the meantime, because it's at the photo shop, too." Which meant Dad wouldn't have his gift for Christmas.

"We'll think on it." Johanna pushed away from the door frame with a determined nod. "We'll figure out something."

"But what?" Meg bit her bottom lip. "Any ideas?"

"Not one." Chelsea shook her head, only that

she would walk to town if she had to. It might take her all day, but she'd do it. After breakfast.

She followed the scent of frying bacon and simmering coffee into the kitchen. Dee bounded into the living room with a good-morning bark. Burt deigned to greet her with a glance as he sat at the living room windowsill, peering through the thickly falling snow. Johanna hadn't been kidding. A good foot or more of new accumulation covered the landscape and the road.

Definitely, no driving to town and no seeing Michael. Disappointment rocked her with a force not even she could deny.

"My dream of a white Christmas came true," Sara Beth called from the kitchen. "I just didn't want it to be quite so white."

"No kidding." Chelsea followed Dee into the kitchen, where the scent of sizzling bacon made her stomach growl. Bayley looked up from his bed in the corner and blinked a hello. She knelt to rub his soft head. But where were her thoughts? On Michael. He lived in town, he'd likely be able to make it to the clinic. "Where's Dad?"

"Is he still out at the barn spoiling the horses?" Meg asked as she sauntered into the kitchen, ponytail swinging.

"You know Dad and horses." Johanna skirted the breakfast bar with two steaming coffee mugs in hand. "Okay, the apple doesn't fall far from the tree in this family."

"Thanks, Jo." Chelsea relieved her sister of a coffee mug and took a bracing sip. Much better. Now that her brain was working, she noticed blueberry muffins cooling on the counter and Sara Beth scrambling eggs in a bowl. The kitchen table gleamed with Mom's holiday dishes. "Remember when we would get up before dawn, squealing down the hall waking everyone up?"

"It was me," Meg spoke up, skating on her socks into the room. "I was the squealer."

"And we'd race down the stairs," Sara Beth remembered, adding a handful of cheese to her mixing bowl. "Still in our jammies."

"And Mom would follow after us, yawning and tying her robe." Johanna handed the second coffee cup to Meg. "Dad would grab the camera and start clicking."

"All the presents under the tree just waiting for us, wrapped with ribbons and bows." Meg took a sip.

"Mom made every present look special." Chelsea circled around the island. "My favorite Christmas was when all the presents were opened and Mom said there was one more gift waiting for me in the barn."

"Rio." Sara Beth remembered fondly. "It was the same way with my Aurora. We shuffled out to the barn with our pajamas under our coats. There she was waiting for me in her stall."

"I'd figured out the pattern when my turn came," Meg confessed as she sipped her coffee. "So after the last present was unwrapped, I was ready to pop with excitement. Mom turned to Dad and said, 'Grant, I think that's all the gifts.' And Dad said, 'No, there's still one last one. Now, where did we leave it?'"

"And you shouted, 'It's in the barn.'" Chelsea checked the sizzling bacon. "I think you ran so fast you were a blur."

"Probably," Meg agreed. "My handsome Charles was waiting for me in his stall. He saw me charging down the aisle, so he leaned over the rail as if he couldn't wait for me to hug him. It was love at first sight."

"It was the same with my Ranger." Johanna tore paper towels from the roll and folded them. "Christmas is the season for love. All kinds of love, including horse love."

"And especially sister love." Chelsea grabbed the tongs and dropped a slice of crisp bacon on the paper towel to drain. "There's nothing like it."

"Amen." Sara Beth sidled up close, bowl in hand, and poured the egg mixture into the waiting pan.

"I have the greatest sisters ever." Johanna carried a plate of muffins to the table.

"That's what I was going to say." Meg opened the fridge and pulled out a carton of orange juice. Laughter peppered the air as their conversation turned to the upcoming pie-making schedule for later in the morning.

Chelsea plucked another bacon slice from the fry pan and wished she wasn't thinking of Michael.

"Are you sure?" Kate Koffman's face went snow-white. Down the hospital corridor the nurses began singing "We Wish You A Merry Christmas."

It was going to be a very merry Christmas for the Koffmans. He gave thanks for that. "Kelsey is in remission. Just when we thought it was never going to happen, she surprised us."

"That's, oh, that's—" Tears filled Kate's eyes and she choked. Her husband drew her into his arms, holding her as she wept with joy.

This was what made his job worth it. When a child beat the odds and a family stayed together, bound by love and hope. It reminded him that every day was a miracle, a day the Lord had made. Something that should never be taken for granted.

He glanced around the doorway at the little girl tucked in bed, playing a board game. Grandma Koffman swiped tears from her eyes, she must have been listening at the door. "Merry Christmas Eve, Kelsey."

"Merry Christmas Eve, Dr. Mike." She moved her shoe token four squares. "I got all the railroads."

"Excellent. Those are my favorites, too." He pulled a small gift from his white coat pocket and set it on the foot of her bed. "Something from me, my daughter helped pick it out. Your dad tells me we'd better get you discharged before they close every last road in town. You don't want to spend Christmas Eve stuck here."

"Nope. I wanna go *home*." Her eyes brightened at the word.

"Your wish is my command, Princess Kelsey," he said. That reminded him of the sleigh ride and of Chelsea snuggled warmly against him in the sleigh with her pretty alto lilting in the wind and snowflakes falling all around her. The affection in him became an unbearable pain of longing and loss wrapped up together. He braced his hands on the foot rail, trying to hide it, waiting for the pain to pass.

It didn't. It hadn't since Chelsea had sailed out of the hospital chapel, glad to be just friends. No, that wasn't accurate. She didn't want another bad experience with romance, and he didn't blame her. He'd tried as hard as he could with his marriage, but he and Diana had never had the effortless bond his parents had, or the one he'd always wanted.

"Let's get going, girl!" Kate Koffman sailed into the room, her lashes damp from her tears and a smile as big as the moon. "We have an adventure ahead of us. They've closed Grimes Road. Our road might be next."

Chelsea lived just off Grimes Road at the end of Wild Rose Lane. Did that mean she hadn't come into the clinic this morning? He'd come straight to the hospital because of Kelsey, but he'd meant to stop by the office and thank her again for the kitten basket.

When he finally had a few Macie-free minutes to open it, he'd been surprised at what she'd found. Chelsea could blame her sisters all she wanted, but she couldn't fool him. He knew she had picked out the dozen new cat toys, the top-of-the-line kitten bed not to mention the fuzzy kitty slippers and a purple Sunshine Animal Clinic T-shirt, both in Macie's size.

A cell phone beeped—not his. Kate wrapped her daughter in a hug, kissed the top of her head and pulled out her phone. "Chelsea just messaged me asking if there was anything she could do for us today."

"Such a caring doctor." Grandma Koffman spoke up. "She's been a good friend to you, Kate."

"Just when I needed one most," Kate agreed,

tapping away on her keys. "I can't believe she's coming into town today. She lives farther out than we do."

He believed it. That was Chelsea. His chest squeezed so hard his ribs ached. She was always doing for others, her friends, her family, her church and sick kids. It only made him love her more. Of course he loved her.

He left the Koffmans to their preparations and wished them safe driving. Whiteout conditions met him the instant he stepped foot outside. He batted snow out of his eyes as he hiked to the doctor's lot, beeped open his SUV and dug out his ice scraper all the while thinking of Chelsea. A stubborn layer of ice coated his windshield, so he popped into the car, shivering even as the defroster blasted hot air on high and waited for it to make a dent in the ice.

His work had always been the source of conflict with Diana, the reason why he'd disappointed Diana so much. He'd compromised as much as he could on his work hours, but he'd never been able to leave pediatric oncology, the way she'd asked. She'd been unhappy with who he was, and that was something he'd tried but couldn't change. He'd done the best he could, and he may never be brilliant at relationships, but he'd done okay. Macie was thriving and happy again and when he was with Chelsea, everything felt *right*. Perfect. Meant to be.

The week had been agony without her, so he pulled out his phone. Did he text or call? Texting would be easier on his aching heart, but he pressed her phone number instead. Static crackled in his ear. One ring, two rings. Maybe she'd made it in despite the road report and was busy at the clinic.

"Hello?" Wind whistled across the connection. "Michael?"

"It sounds like I caught you outside." He leaned back against the cool seat, thinking of her smile. His day wasn't the same without it.

"Yes, you could say I'm outside. Kate texted the good news. They got a miracle just in time for Christmas." She sounded a little out of breath. And what was that faint crunching sound?

"Yes, they did. Chelsea, are you outside walking in the snow?"

"Something like that. The road to town is closed, so I'm heading out to saddle up Rio." The wind whistled harder, making it tough to hear.

"Are you trying to come in to work today?"

"No, Steve called to tell me not to try. Susan is filling in, since she lives in town." She sounded breezy, an independent woman who didn't need anyone. "I've just got an errand to run."

"It must be important to go out in a storm like

this." Wind gusted the side of his SUV, reminding him of the near whiteout conditions.

"We have one last Christmas gift to pick up, so we're doing it the old-fashioned way, right, Sara Beth?" In the background someone answered, her words muffled by the driving snowfall, the creak of a door and boots stomping on concrete. "Hey, right now we could be sisters in the eighteen hundreds heading to town on horseback."

"That's right," came Sara Beth's distant reply. "Let's hope you don't have to say the same thing if the power goes out because of the storm. I'm partial to modern-day electricity."

"Me, too," he agreed, not to be left out of the conversation. Horses nickering in the background told him they'd reached the barn. He remembered why their trip was so important. Her father's Christmas present was still in town, at the only photo shop in Sunshine, Wyoming. "And you're riding what, five miles, in the middle of a whiteout? Anyone else would wait until the storm was over. Chelsea, I've never known anyone more stubborn than you."

"Yes, but stubborn is a good quality. It can mean tenacious, dedicated, and able to see anything through. That's not so bad, right?"

"Right." It also meant unfaltering, dedicated and committed. They were so alike, him and Chelsea. Two sides of the same coin. They belonged together, he knew it now beyond all doubt. He could feel the certainty in his soul. "Are you taking the road or some shortcut to town?"

"—take—ild Rose La—ay—off—kit—" Static drowned her out and the connection went dead.

He couldn't get it back.

Chapter Seventeen

Snow tumbled from an unforgiving sky, icy against her cheek as Chelsea reined Rio down the solemn stretch of white drifts that buried the country road. The thick and encompassing veil of falling snow cut off all sight of the surrounding countryside. No sign of other houses or horse stables, and only the swoop of the telephone lines laden with snow and the occasional mailbox or fence post sticking up out of the whiteness reminded her they weren't alone.

"You've been quiet." Sara Beth's words were muffled by the scarf covering half of her face. "You're thinking about him, aren't you?"

"And trying not to." Without him, the world didn't seem as kind or as colorful. A bitter north wind blasted hard, and she shivered. He'd called to check up on her, like a good friend.

"You miss him." Sara Beth seemed to already

know the truth, the one Chelsea had been fighting ever since Michael had helped her into the sleigh that day.

"This past week has been terrible. There, I admitted it." The confession felt torn from her. "I've tried everything I can to keep from feeling this way."

"But it hasn't helped." Sara Beth nodded sympathetically. "Sometimes God puts a love in your heart, Chelsea. One that is everlasting."

"No, Michael isn't the one. He's closed off, he can be like granite one minute and you have no idea what he's thinking. But then he goes and does something so thoughtful and giving." She shook her head, her emotions too tangled up to make any sense, but she knew one thing. "Kind and giving. That's number one on my list."

"Right, the Perfect Man list." Sara Beth swiped snowflakes from her eyelashes. "What's number two?"

"A good sense of humor. Not that it's obvious at first, Michael comes across as so serious." She blinked snow off her eyelashes, remembering her first impression of him, steel and fury when he'd protectively tried to shield his daughter from her in the cemetery. Or her first day at the clinic when he'd towered over her like a pillar of cool granite. "But he can be so funny. My kind of humor, you know?"

"Sure," Sara Beth agreed, switching the reins to her other gloved hand and jamming the cold one into her jacket pocket. "You two seem to laugh when you're together. What's number three?"

Was it her imagination, or did the wind have a faintly jingling sound? A gust howled by, swirling snow down the last stretch of Wild Rose Lane. Chelsea took a breath, imagining the typed list, the one she'd written ages ago.

"He has to love me as much as I love him." There, she'd said it and she was afraid Michael didn't love her that way, that no one could. He'd sat on the pew in the chapel calmly saying he didn't want to take one step farther with her. And she'd agreed just as sensibly.

Except she'd been wrong. She didn't have the courage to tell him the truth. She couldn't even be honest with herself. "I wish I could go back and do this last week differently."

"I know you, Chelsea." Sara Beth stopped to listen to the wind and shook her head. "I thought I heard something. Anyway, I know you would go back in time if you could and say no when Michael asked you into his and Macie's sleigh. That way you wouldn't be here hurting. I hate that you're hurting."

"Me, too." Sara Beth was right, she thought, not liking that about herself. Had she become so careful in life that she'd closed herself up to opportunities? If she had said no, then she never would have zipped across the snow in a sleigh singing Christmas carols or laughed and dreamed and fallen in love with a man who felt like her other half.

A silvery chime rose above the whoosh of howling wind, but the worsening storm gave no hint of what it might be. Icy flecks beat against her face as she peered into the pummeling snow. Was that a faint shadow? A flash of pink? The shadow became two horses plowing through the drifts and a little girl's pink coat. But it was the man seated beside her that stole her breath.

Michael.

"What are you doing here?" She nearly slipped off her horse. Her mittens grabbed the saddle horn, keeping her upright. She blinked, and he was still there, not her imagination, not her wishful thinking, the man she adored. "It's nearly a blizzard, in case you hadn't noticed."

"Right. I figured if you were out in it, I could be too." He waited for the sleigh to skid to a stop and ignored Natalie, who listened intently as she held the reins in the front seat. "Macie loves sleigh riding and I thought she might want a ride for Christmas."

"Hi, Chelsea. Hi, Sara Beth." Macie waved, bundled up happily on the seat. "We're going on another adventure."

"Where to this time, Princess Macie?" Chelsea

leaned closer, her face pink from the cold but her blue gaze alight with affection for his girl. "Are you off to see more polar bears?"

"I thought about it." When Chelsea's mare pushed her nose into Macie's hand, the girl happily stroked it. "And I'd like to see the penguins again, but this time we're on a Christmas mission."

"Not to the North Pole, I hope. Word is this storm could get worse. Blizzard warnings are up for afternoon. That's why we're getting to town while we can."

"That's why we're out, too." He spoke up, wishing Chelsea would look at him. He steeled his spine, gathering his courage. She'd didn't want anything serious, but seeing her again and hearing her voice was the balm he'd needed. This past week without her, with only distant glimpses and friendly hellos had been torture. No, he'd prefer torture compared with a single day of living without her. He braced his feet, sure of his course and afraid he was heading for heartbreak. "We're headed to your house."

"Our house?" Her gaze locked on his. She hadn't guessed. She didn't know. Surprise twisted her pretty mouth. "Why? I mean, you should be home getting ready for Christmas. Maybe paying a visit to Mrs. Collins."

"My mom is out doing that right now," he

assured her. "Two little Christmas gifts will be safe at her house tonight."

"What little Christmas gifts?" Macie interjected. "Are they for me?"

"You'll have to wait and see." He tugged the brim of his daughter's knit hat to cover her ears. "Maybe both presents are for me."

"No way." Chelsea's gentle quip rang like music. "Not unless they are two pieces of coal."

"See? They are for me," Macie sang happily.

Chelsea towered above him, dappled with white. Snow dotted her hat, clung in her wavy hair and crested the slender line of her shoulders. She sat straight in her saddle, as sweet as a holiday dream.

His dream.

Full of hope, he stood to offer her his hand. "Why don't you ride with us? It's warmer beneath the fleece blankets."

"I'd like that." The truth hovered in the promise of her smile. "But we have to get to town."

"No, you don't." His fingers grasped hers and held on tight. "I picked up your father's Christmas gift."

"You did *what?*"

"Couldn't help myself. It's the way things are going to be." It was a promise made to be kept, one that would never waver. "From this point on, I'm here for you. Always and forever. Come, let me take you home."

"Uh—" *No* was her automatic response. No to his help, no to his offer, no to always and forever. Chelsea bit her bottom lip as she thought, realizing that was her fear talking, the part of her that never wanted to take a risk and step off her planned course. Had her whole life become playing it safe and saying no to wonderful possibilities? What would she miss out on if she said no?

With all the emotion swirling around in her, she tried to cling to what was real. "Y-you have Dad's gift?"

"Right here in the sleigh." He patted a big and bulky object strapped to the seat beside Natalie, wrapped in plastic.

"Why did you do this?" Tears burned behind her eyes, tears she refused to let fall. There could be only one reason why, and it frightened her as much as she wished for it.

"Because I love you." His hand holding hers wasn't the only connection between them.

"You l-love me?" she repeated because the words didn't sink in. They were sudden and shocking and real and everything she wanted.

"I do." He tugged, she slid off Rio's back and landed light as air in his strong arms. "You are impossible not to love, Chelsea McKaslin. I never thought any woman could open my heart like this, but you did it with one smile. Just one. That's all it took."

"I didn't mean to." The confession rolled across her lips, one that made him grin. Not fair, since she had no defense against the power of his dimples.

"I know this might not be what you want to hear. I know this isn't the right time for you." His words rumbled through her like a prayer, sweet and solemn. He really did love her. His gaze deepened, showing all of his soul. "I'll wait as long as it takes. I don't want to stand in the way of your dreams. I'm hoping one day we can reach some of those dreams together. What do you say?"

Devotion to him welled up with a force so strong her will couldn't stop it. Logic couldn't diminish it, nothing could. God had put this in her heart, this rare and perfect affection. Like nothing she'd known before, like nothing she would ever know again. No way could she let this opportunity pass, not a second time. She believed in Michael. She had faith that he would never let her down.

"I don't want you to wait for me." She laid her hand on his chest, her heart so full she could hardly speak. "I don't want to waste any more time. I love you, Michael."

"You do? That is the best Christmas gift I could ever want." Relief dug into the pleasant creases of his face, making him even more handsome. He caressed the side of her cheek with a touch so tender, the only thing more sweet was the brush of his lips to hers.

Their first kiss was fairy-tale perfect, just like their love would be. Snow swirled around them, like pieces of heavenly grace. Sleigh bells jingled faintly, as if brushed by a loving hand, a musical approval as Michael broke their kiss and pulled her into his arms where she was meant to be.

Forever.

Epilogue

Christmas Morning

The Christmas lights cast a vivid glow over the four sisters seated in a half circle around the tree. A fire crackled in the fireplace, soft instrumental hymns lilted from the CD player and Burt purred contently from the back of the couch.

"It's perfect, just perfect." Grant stared at the framed portrait of his daughters, once young and sweet, and now so beautiful. Just like their mother. "Seeing your mom smiling like this is the best gift I could ask for."

His four girls beamed happily as he leaned the frame against the wall. Dee and Bayley watched curiously from their places beside the hearth. "We'll hang it after the rest of the presents are opened. Johanna, you're next, love."

"Let's see." She rose up on her knees, peering

in at the plentiful piles of festive wrapping and ribbon. "That's easy. I pick Mom's."

"Good choice," Chelsea agreed with a nod. She sorted through a few packages, came up with a square box and squinted at the tag. "No, this is Meg's."

"Gimme." With a grin, Meg stretched out both hands to take her mother's last gift.

"Sara Beth's," Chelsea read, nudging the next box across the carpet. "Here's mine. And yours, Johanna."

"Let's open them together." Johanna's eyes glistened as she untied the frilly bow. "We already know what they are."

"She got us each the same one," Meg agreed, untying her gift's bow.

Chelsea tackled the scotch tape and the wrapping paper fell away. The box held a porcelain ornament, one of a young mother with a small daughter on her lap, reading the Christmas story. No one spoke as they admired their gifts, and the living room fell silent. Chelsea understood the message of her mother's gift, that wherever Mom was, she loved them still.

"We love you, too, Mom." She would always miss her mother, but her love was stronger than her grief. The brilliant glory of the Christmas tree, the peaceful sunny Christmas morning and the faces of her family reminded her of all her blessings. Life really was beautiful.

Dee lifted her head off her paws and barked. Bayley gave a welcoming woof. Boots clomped up the porch steps and knocked on the door.

"I may have forgotten to mention something." Sara Beth smiled mischievously. "When Michael and Macie brought us home in the sleigh yesterday, I invited them to Christmas breakfast hoping the county would be able to plow the roads, which they apparently did. I thought it was fitting."

"Very fitting," Meg and Johanna agreed in unison, but Chelsea was already on her feet, her hand turning the doorknob, breathlessly eager to see the man she loved.

"Merry Christmas." Michael towered above her, his granite face gentle when he gazed upon her.

"Merry Christmas." She was against him with his arms folded strong around her. Tucked against his chest, she didn't notice the icy air. Not one bit. She could hold him like this forever, stay cuddled against him, safe and sweet, but a patter of footsteps on the porch behind him caught her attention.

"Look what I got for Christmas." Macie balanced a pink carrier as if it held the greatest treasure. "I didn't just get Pearl. I got Hank, too!"

"I didn't want to leave them home alone,"

Michael explained, and yesterday Sara Beth hinted it would be all right to bring them along."

"Absolutely. We are animal people here." Chelsea stepped aside to allow father and daughter into the warm house and closed the door. Her sisters rushed forward, the carrier was opened and two adorable little kittens mewed their greetings as they were held and adored and snuggled. Dee tapped over to inspect them with a welcoming tail wag.

Chelsea couldn't take her gaze off Michael. After the sleigh had returned them home and he'd carried Dad's gift upstairs for Sara Beth to wrap, the two of them had talked about everything. Their feelings, their future and even marriage.

"There's something I want to give you." He pulled her away from her family and into the light of the Christmas tree. He fished a small black velvet box from his pocket. "I had Natalie swing the sleigh by the jewelry store on our way home yesterday. Macie helped me pick this one. She liked the blue stone because it matched your eyes."

A two-caret sapphire winked up at her, rimmed with baguette diamonds. Her breath caught. Stunned, surprised, overjoyed, she forgot to breathe.

"Marry me, Chelsea." Warmth, humor, love and commitment layered his voice as he went down on one knee. In the background her sisters gasped,

Macie smiled and Michael's hand closed over her own. "You fill my heart like no one ever has. You bring color to my world and joy to my life. Please give me the best Christmas gift of all and agree to be my wife."

"I will." No panic, no fear, only great happiness filled her as he slid the ring on her finger. Vaguely she heard Dee barking, Macie hopping up and down and her sisters cheering, but Michael stood front and center. The promise to love and cherish her shone like a sacred vow in his gaze. A vow she could trust.

It was easy to see a future, one she could believe in, one that would last. Of happy days to come filled with their work as doctors, of raising Macie and adding more children to their family one day. She pictured their house full of little girls laughing and gathering around a future Christmas tree. "I love you so much, Michael."

"I love you more." He cradled the back of her neck with one hand, holding her close as their lips met. His kiss was perfection, proof this wasn't just any ordinary love. This was what she dreamed love could be. Two hearts, one soul. Happily ever after. Forever and ever.

"Hey, what about the rest of our presents?" Meg asked, cradling a snuggling Hank.

"I have a lot more stuff to open," Johanna

added, tucking an adorable Pearl under her chin. "C'mon, Macie, you can help us."

"Okay!" Macie slipped one hand in Chelsea's and held on so tight. Together they settled on the floor in the light of the Christmas tree, laughing and talking and opening gifts, a happy family.

* * * * *

Dear Reader,

Welcome back to another McKaslin story. As you may have guessed by now, I love few things more than writing a Christmas story. It is one of my favorite times of year, with twinkling lights and Christmas cookies and carols celebrating family, love and faith. So it felt appropriate to have chosen a Christmas story for the McKaslin cousins who live in snowy Wyoming. Chelsea has worked hard to become a pediatrician but has yet to discover that God has planned greater dreams for her than she could ever dream for herself. Those dreams happen to come in the form of Michael Kramer, a dedicated doctor and father whose heart comes alive when he meets beautiful Chelsea. I hope you enjoy the wonder of falling in love along with Chelsea and Michael and that your Christmas season is filled with love.

Thank you for choosing *Jingle Bell Bride* and for returning to the McKaslin family with me.

Wishing you a blessed and beautiful holiday season,

Jillian Hart

Questions for Discussion

1. What are your first impressions of Michael? How would you describe his character?

2. What are your first impressions of Chelsea? What do you learn about her from the way she treats Macie, Michael and her family? What does this tell you about her character?

3. Chelsea has taken to heart the Bible passage that a man chooses his path and God directs his (or her) steps. What does this say about her? Do you think she's right?

4. How does Michael feel about Chelsea at the beginning of the book? How does this change as he spends time with her?

5. Why do you think Chelsea is afraid to take risks with her heart?

6. What kind of doctor is Michael? What does this say about his character?

7. What does Chelsea learn about herself? What does Michael learn about himself through the course of the story?

8. What role does family play in the book?

9. Both Chelsea and Michael are wrestling with grief and a sense of guilt. How does Chelsea resolve this? How does Michael let go?

10. What values do you think are important in this book?

11. What do you think are the central themes in this book? How do they develop? What meanings do you find in them?

12. How does God guide both Chelsea and Michael? How is this evident? How does God lead them to true love?

13. There are many different kinds of love in this book. What are they? What do Chelsea and Michael each learn about true love?

Get 2 Free Books,
Plus 2 Free Gifts—
just for trying the Reader Service!

Get 2 Free Books,
Plus 2 Free Gifts—
just for trying the Reader Service!